A preview…

Homo Thug

By

Asante Kahari

Published by

Harlem Book Center, Inc.
129 West 137th Street, 1B
New York, NY 10030
Tel: +1/646-739-6429

Warning!
This is work of fiction. All the characters, incidents and dialogues are the products of the author's imagination and are not to be construed as real. Any references or similarities to actual events, entities, real people, living or dead, or to real locales are intended to give the novel a sense of reality. Any similarity in other names, characters, entities, places and incidents is purely coincidental.

ISBN:978-0-9800822-3-4

AUTHOR'S ACKNOWLEDGEMENTS

This will not take very long. I want to thank Sidi, the publisher, for being ever so patient with me. (Asante kahari-NYS ID 85807350804 @690Gates Ave.Apt 5F,NY,NY11221, asantekahari@verizon.net 347-351-7343,home 718-443-0011).To Carmen Garrett, when my wife and I needed you the most you were always there. To Bernadette Jackson and Omar. Omar, your wife is a weirdo, just kidding, her MSW degree has blurred her vision. She is too damn idealistic. To Paulette, Nitivia, and Jaquasia, you are the worst neighbors in the world. Paulette Clemmons, you are not the next American Idol. Slow your role Grandma. T.D and LaShae Green, you guys are the best, well at least T.D. is. Your Wife is crazy. To the Jackson family, I know you don't like me but for the sake of your daughter you tolerate me. Uncle John, I love you dearly. To my Little Brother Danyule, I am amazed at what a man you have become. I love you very much, even when I can't show it. To my brother Troy and nephew Idris Mitchell, I know the power of love; you don't have to tell me, I feel it. Bilal and Sharon Carter. My sisters Jillian, Natosha, and Shanel, I would give a right arm to show you how much you truly mean to me. Kevin, there is a special bond I share with you that can't be explained. I worry about you even in my dreams. Jr, you are my brother. You can't choose your siblings, I wish I could. Akmir Grey, Otis Williams, Don Miller and Barbara, AKA Busy B. You have been more than a mother to me. Bobby and Tommy, love you dearly. I miss Gloria, Uncle William and Aunt Louise everyday. Shatae, Joyce and Tianna. Joyce we have been down this road before. I love you more than the world has water. Renee, Bobby, Michael, Ebony,Jamal, family is family. I have far too many uncles and aunts to name. Uncle Kenny, Trish, and Nate. The rest of you can charge it to my head. Don's wife Mel, Yaz, Whip, Diamond, China, DeNita, Steve Hall, Jeffrey Sledge, Diane Lee, I can't be sorry enough for the wrong I have committed against you, I am still paying for it. Nikki Jones and Family. Octavia Kahari, love you. Last but not least, to my wife, Olivia. I don't know where I would be had it not been for you. I still wonder why you keep on believing, keep on loving, keep on sharing. I know the love of God because I see it in your face every morning. If I forgot you it was probably intentional. Just because you are someone's friend doesn't necessarily mean that view you as the same. I am learning that slowly but surely.

Homo Thug

By

Asante Kahari

CHAPTER TWELVE

I had been on the streets for a couple of months with no success at finding gainful employment. No one would hire me because of my criminal conviction. Each time I would apply for a job, I would be denied because of it. I decided that today was going to be my last day trying to make it right by being a productive citizen in society.

Diane was trying the best she could to get her father to hire me in whatever capacity he could but he want budging. The money I had came home with was gone damn near the week I got out, me and Diane was partying like it was 1999. Every now and then I would go into Ava's beauty shop and cut a few heads but I wasn't really feeling it. The started me out with a few days as a favor to keep parole off of my back. I was getting cool with everyone in the shop, especially Precious and Toni. I knew they wanted me to fuck the shit out of them but I wasn't paying that any mind. They kept trying to invite me to this club across the bridge called the Quarry. I had heard from the other girls in the shop that that was not the type of club that I wanted to be fucking around in.

I kept putting Precious and Toni off telling them I would go week after week. I felt a degree of loyalty to both of them because they both would give me paper every chance they got. It was as if they were baiting me so that I could bless them with some dick. They had no inclination that I had dabbled in prison so I had no reason to believe they were acting out of some prior knowledge about me, they just had a craving for me and thought they might have a shot if they were nice to me. All faggots get off trying to turn somebody out that they believe is straight, it's the only way to validate their sexuality.

My aunt knew I was fucked up and starting giving me the money back in small pieces every morning before I left for a job interview or canvassing for one. When I woke up this morning there was a note on the table with some Hi Ho crackers, and a fifty dollar bill wishing me luck on my search today. Luck or not, this was it for me, I was tired of the let downs.

I went outside and got a Daily News. I was going to hit as many job agencies as possible. Every agency I went to made me fill out a long questionnaire. I wouldn't even make it past the next phase because the moment they saw the box checked off about me having a felony conviction, the moment they would come up with an excuse as to why I would not be a right fit, I thought there were laws against shit like that. Since this was it for me, I thought I would walk and canvass the whole of the city on foot. I walked all the way downtown by city hall; I mostly walked because I wanted to see the world around me, I was home for a few months but I was still enjoying my freedom. I saw a sign directly in back of city hall that read," New York city Housing authority is looking for you." I decided to go in and have a look see, maybe they were looking for me. I went upstairs to the housing administration floor, it was packed with niggers waiting to be seen for an interview. I was the only nigger there with a suit on and a resume in hand. I knew I was on my way. Today just might be my lucky day.

I went up to the front desk and was immediately asked by the receptionist. "Are you here for the employment fair for housing?'

"Yes ma'am, I am," I replied.

"Then I am going to need you to fill out this application and questionnaire form and when your name is called, follow the green line to the door that says interview."

I filled out the questionnaire and application and returned it to her. I was called about a half an hour later. I followed the green line and saw the sign in front of a lady's office by the name of Mrs. Delaney. She was a beautiful black woman with big luscious lips that you would want to kiss all over.

"Mr. Fraser, I have briefly looked over your application

and I see you have an associates degree in liberal arts and a bachelors in business administration. Are you sure you're applying for the right job? I mean, there are other positions in our organization that can accommodate and utilize your skills."

I was thinking to myself, *I know this but I want to shoot low so they would have no reason to tell me no.*

"The maintenance position is perfect for me right now Mrs. Delaney. As you can see, I am more than qualified to sweep floors and mop hallways."

She looked astonished at my reply and responded in the affirmative. "Can't argue with that…well, I guess that settles that. When can you start?"

Shit. Start? I guess she was telling me I got the job. You don't ask a nigger when he can start if you have no intention of hiring him.

"As soon as possible," I replied.

"Okay, be at this address on Monday morning, 9:00 a.m. sharp."

I was excited as hell. I landed a job.

"Thank you ma'am. Thank you very much."

The interview is apparently over there. I rise to leave the office, ecstatic as can be at my good fortune. Just as I reached the door, the unthinkable comes.

"Oh, Mr. Fraser. I'll just need you to sign here and check box number sixteen."

Shit, I knew it was too damn good to be true. We all know what box number sixteen was. I hesitantly took the application and checked off yes and handed it back for inspection and final approval. She looks it over and her expression changes from one of excitement to one of disappointment.

"Mr. Fraser, I'm very sorry but the city's policies state that any individual hired for a city agency position must have a clean record." I was floored. I pleaded.

"Mrs. Delaney, what am I supposed to do? If the city doesn't want to hire me, what can I expect from the private sector? If I can't sweep your floors, whose floors can I sweep? Tell me that Mrs. Delaney?" her response was the same as before.

"Mr. Fraser, I'm sorry, but those are the rules and policies. I'm so sorry."

"Yeah, me too," I responded in disgust. I turned my back on her and headed out the office. I felt like Al Pacino in the Godfather.

The more I tried to get out of the life of crime. The more I was inadvertently being pulled back in. If no one was going to give me a chance, then I was going to take a chance and create the American dream for myself. There was no way I was going to starve out here.

I went to a pay phone on the corner, in front of the building and decided to pull out my ace in the hole. I still had Rico's number but I was holding back because I thought I could make it without doing the wrong thing, I was sadly mistaken.

Crime was my only option at this point, and if I was going to venture back into the life of crime, I might as well do it with all of my heart. On the other end of the receiver was the familiar voice I needed to hear, it was Rico. I told him of my desire to get paid.

"Yo Ric, its your boy back from the penal. You gave me your number a couple of months ago with an offer to make things happen if I wanted in. Well now I want in."

He was all too happy to hear those words. "My nigger, this is your lucky day. We have an initiation in about two hours at the spot. Can you make it?"

I was thinking to myself, what kind of initiation? But I was desperate so whatever it was I was down for it.

"Yeah, I can make it, just give me the address."

I pull out my pen and a piece of paper to record what he was telling me, 950 West 120th Street. I told him I was heading up there right now. I jumped on the train and headed uptown to the address. I got on the 6 train to the Times Square then took the shuttle to the A train. I got off at 125th Street, a block away from Eighth Avenue.

When I got out of the station, I pulled out the paper that I had written the address on. It was in walking distance so I headed to the address walking down Morningside Avenue. When I got to 120th Street I realized that I was already in the 900 buildings. It was apparent that it was his block. What type of operation was he running in one of these houses? The building was a nice looking brownstone. I knocked on the door and someone came to the peephole and looked at me with a piercing look that indicated he was checking me out for something. Behind the door, someone answers my request for admission via my knock on the door. "Who?"

"It's Michael," I replied. "Is Rico there?"

There was a slight pause. The peephole slides shut and several locks are unlocked. The door fillies open and Rico is standing there looking at me like someone he hadn't seen in a lifetime. For a split second, my mind began to flashback to the times when we were kids in sparford. I thought about the young Puerto Rican that let Tislam fuck the shit out of him without ceasing. I thought about how weak he was then and how strong he is now. He was defiantly a homosexual, but he was no sucker and you could see that. He was a homosexual thug nigger. I didn't see an ounce of punk in him as I stood there. In fact, I saw nothing but strength and a high level of respect from his comrades. I wondered, how could that be me if they know his past and what happened to him as a kid, or probably as an adult? It didn't matter to me at that point, his sins were forgiven in my book, shit I was just as guilty. I was a homo in my own way. I guess we both had demons. His yell jolted me back to reality.

"Mike! Snap out of it."

"Yeah, its me in the flesh."

He drags me into the house where the rest of his homeboys were. Behind me I could hear the reinforced door lock. I am taken to a side room where he wants to discuss some things with me before he reintroduces me to the rest of his click. I met three of them gangster unit niggers at Webster Hall my first night home. Rico looked like he was bracing to tell me something he knew I would not accept. He said that everyone of the members of his click had done it and there were no exceptions. I listened to his explanation.

"We have an initiation that ensures every man down with us keeps a secret. It is a secret that ruin a man and a secret that is shared by all of us so that no man is above the crew. I thought of it, and it is also a way for me to hide the sin of what Tislam did to me back in the day. Every nigger down with us has to fuck somebody in the crew. In doing so, we have something on you, and you have something on us. We are all men by virtue of our shared secret. What someone can know about you, they can also know about me. You telling on someone in the crew is like telling on yourself."

I looked at him with sincerity and shared my sentiments

on the matter. "Are you fucking crazy? Do you think I would entertain letting somebody fuck me up the ass?" he didn't feel the least bit slighted.

"You are definitely welcome to leave, and there will be no hard feelings. But I got a move that we all are about to make that is going to set all of us straight for the rest of our lives. Oh yeah. Don't think I don't know what you were doing while you were on lock down. I know Dee Dee real well. He was down with us before he died. He told me everything."

I was stunned. Dee Dee was dead and this motherfucker knew about the shit I did to Dee Dee. I knew it was no bullshit, how else would he know that me and Dee Dee had any connection unless he really did speak with him. I had to confront the issue. I could either lie and get on the defensive or I could come out with it and confirm his statement. If I was going to confirm it I might as well take him up on his offer. He already knew I was involved in activity that' wasn't kosher. I decided to keep it on the up and up with him. After all, he was in the same ball park so to speak.

"You know what, I am not even going to lie about it, I need to get it out in the open anyway, at least to somebody. You know how it is on lock down. I just wanted to feel the touch of a woman and Dee Dee was the closest thing to one. I kept your secret a secret and I hope you can keep mine."

He interjected. "Dog, I didn't bring it up because I am a better than you. I got fucked as a kid but I am still a man and I don't have any ill feelings for Tislam. In a lot of ways he taught me how to be strong. I do think you are missing out on an opportunity to get some real paper. But once again, rules are rules so if you want to get down I suggest you think about it."

Shit, what real choice did I have? I didn't have shit, and my cover was blown. I might as well get something out of the deal. I had to know one thing though. It was killing me.

"What happened to Dee Dee. How did he die?"

He looked at me with a sadness that represented a secret all his own. "He died of pneumonia."

What a relief, I thought to myself. *At least it wasn't AIDS.*

My turns face turned from one of anxiety to one of relief. Fuck it. I had nothing to lose and everything to gain. If this move was anything like he was hyping it up to be, then I was on.

"I am going to take you up on your offer, but whatever the move is, I want to call the shots. I think I can do better a job at orchestrating a move than those dudes I saw you with at the club."

"Aight, you got that. Now let me take you inside."

He took me to a smoke filled room with dudes sitting at a round table. They were seated like the knights were seated in the mythical story, king Arthur's court. They are all at the table doing a myriad of tasks. Some are smoking while others are counting mounds of cash. Some are also dispensing vials of crack into plastic bags. Rico prepares them for my introduction.

"Listen up, my niggers. I want to introduce y'all to a long time homey of mine. He is like bone and flesh of my flesh..."

I look at him from the corner of my eye. He continues to give his speech, "He's a G from the heart and we can all learn a lot from him. Mike, this is the clique."

I give them a short, what's up. There is a kid loading bullets with his bare hands. His name was Murder Rob. I had to let him know there was a brighter way to his madness.

"My man, try doing that with gloves, It works."

Rico throws his arms around my shoulders.

"Yo, see what I told y'all motherfuckers? He knows his shit!" he continued his introduction. "You already know Half a Dollar, Young God, and Stop the Bank."

There were other niggers there that he didn't even bother to introduce me to. I guess they weren't as important. He pulled a blindfold out of his pocket and told me to take off my clothes. I almost thought he was going to forget about that initiation bit. Shit, I almost wanted to believe I was being excused from it. I expressed my immediate concerns about the blindfold.

"What the fuck am I being blindfolded for?" I thought it was some sort of set up type shit going into play, maybe he wanted to have me killed because I was the only one in the room that knew about him and Tislam for sure, he eased my concerns.

"The blindfold is so you don't know which one of us is fucking you. That way no one is above or below anyone else. For all you will ever know is that you have been fucked in the presence of all who are present. It could be all of us fucking you or just one, you will never know."

The blindfold is then placed over my eyes and I am led to another room. I am bent over a table and my pants are unfastened and dropped below my knees. There was nothing but silence for about two minutes.

All of a sudden I feel this slippery like substance being placed all over the crack of my ass. It felt like some sort of lubrication. I could feel the sensation of warm, thick object penetrating my anus. After several pumps I knew the object to be stiff cock in my ass. I could feel the person's balls banging against my buttocks as he dug deeper and deeper into my guts. More than one person was drilling me. I could feel the balls on my body. Some were higher up on my ass than others, indicating the person was taller or shorter. I was being gang banged. Niggers were driving their cocks in my Hershey highway.

The pain was unbearable but the feeling was insatiable. I was enjoying the unthinkable. It hurt oh so good. As each person would take his turn sticking his dirty gun in my shitter shoot., I began to feel the sensation of a York Peppermint Patty. It was the sensation of a cool rush of menthol-injected spring waters. I could feel the blood pulsating through their venomous cocks, injecting me with all of their poisons.

This was my first game in the outfield as a catcher but I knew it wouldn't be my last. It was certainly a homeroom for the homo community because I was loving it and if loving it was wrong, I didn't want to be right. Like a bonafide homosexual, this was my coming out day, it was the day I admitted to myself that I had a thing for that manwich meal. I wasn't flaming, I was just infatuated with that polish sausage. That one eyed Cyclops had me right where he wanted me. At that moment there was no room for shame. I was a switch hitter whether I wanted to accept it or not.

The blindfold came off. I was disappointed because I wanted it to last forever. It came as no surprise. Everyone had their pants back on and I could never be able to tell which nigger just served the shit out of me, but I was damn sure going to try to find out. There was a dick that I was sure to remember. His balls touched the groove of my back. He had to be tall. Rico told all of them to line up on the wall and I was to pick three of them to fuck. It would be the completion of my initiation. I chose the three gangster unit niggers. I started with the short one, Half a Dollar. He was stockily built with Half a Dollar tattooed on his back. His mouth looked funny as hell. I would later learn it looked that way because he was shot nine times at close range for some shit he had nothing to do with. He wore those bullet holes like a badge of honor.

I bent him over the table and began pumping the shit out of him. He was straight faced as the character Denzel Washington played in Glory when he was being beaten. I knew he liked it. If he was a woman he would be considered a dead lay.

My next victim was Stop the Bank. He had a laid back kind of look that reminded me of a person trying to hide their true self by acting like a tough guy. He just wasn't believable. I guess that was the main reason I chose him. If I had to have anything on anybody it was going to be him. I made it my business to not only fuck the shit out of him, but to cum in him as ,well.

Young Gun was the best fuck. He was light in the ass with a six pack that gave me a good visual to work with. I made him get on the table and hold his dick while I lift up his legs and fucked him from the front. When I was done, I squirted all over his stomach. He looked at me with disgust but I didn't care. What was he going to do to me? I allowed the initiation process because it was a way for me to test the waters of homosexuality without fear of reprisal. If I was a homo, it was going to be on my terms and I damn sure was not going to allow anyone calling me one. I was going to be thuggish as any nigger that ever walked on two feet but I was going to love going through the back door and having other niggers rod shoved in my bon bons.

Rico came over to me with a white cloth with something inside. He told me to open it. It was a gold plated dagger inside with the inscription, Dagger of Honor. He said there was only one way to get out of this organization. It was either going to be shit on his dick or blood on a niggers knife.

"There is no one man above the crew. There is no one more important to each other more than the people in this room. Not mother, father, sister, son. We die together, fuck together, and kill together. Those that oppose us, fuck um two times."

This nigger was really on some shit. I could see a change in Rico that I knew came from his experience as a child with Tis. He was hell bent on humiliating a motherfucker, almost as retribution for what happened to him. It was so deeply ingrained in his brain that even he couldn't recognize it. I was taken back to the room where the round table was and briefed on his one shot deal scheme to get out of the game. I sat down in the first seat by the door. I guess it was prison instincts. I was going to be the first one in and the first one out should anything jump off. When everyone is seated Rico takes center stage in the room and explains his master plan.

"Aight, here's the deal. It's no secret we all said we wanted to get out of the game and into something more legitimate and suited to our characters. Half and his G-unit crew have been making moves in the industry, trying to break in as a rap group. I figure we could do this last big sting and front them the money to do it for themselves. We will be equal partners with the label. I guess the question to ask is, where are we going to get the money to start a full scale label that can compete with these big labels? The answer is simple. Those guineas in little Italy are planning on hitting a select group of dealers with over fifty kilos of heroin, not coke, but heroin. I can't even count the profit we will make off of some shit like that. It will be enough for all of us to start a legitimate enterprise. We could wash that money in no time by starting film companies, clothing lines, vodka and beer distributorships and anything else we can get our people to believe in. I got an inside flunky on their payroll that gave me the names of the niggers they are going to hit off. If we rob these niggers and sell the drugs wholesale out of town we will still make a killing."

My mind immediately generates questions. I was supposed to ask questions, especially now that I had an un derstanding of the dynamics of what he was planning."

"How do you expect us to do that without bringing all types of heat on ourselves? If anybody is given any work like that, they have to believe they can hold it down."

His answer was quick and slick. "That's all the more reason I need you down on this. You got the mind for pulling it all together. One way or another this is going to happen."

I could see he didn't really think things through to perfection. He got an E for effort and Afor balls. I was in. I had nothing to lose. My job search today let me know where I stood with society. It was now time I made a stand for myself. I agreed, but only if it went down with me mapping it out. Not one single deviation from my plan. I told him what I needed.

"First I am going to need all the information you can get on these cats. I need hang out locations, place of residences, everything."

He responds in the affirmative. I gave him my aunt's address and told him to holla at me when he gets it. We embraced and I rolled out. I was exhausted from being up since the morning, among other things. I got back home to my aunts house and headed straight for my bed. Lying on that bed, staring at the ceiling, I started to reflect on a myriad of things, namely what I had just done. It didn't dawn on me until now that I let a nigger take the only thing from me that was sacred, my manhood. I was struggling with how I should view myself as I relate to the world and the faggots that I grew to despise for their crimes. I was just as guilty as them, if not more. I was a fag in hiding.

I also started to think about the awful situation I was putting Diane in. She was the victim in my web of deceit. What kind of man was I not to tell her? The kind that loved here and wanted to spare her feelings of all the hurt, pain and shame that exposure would bring. What penetrated my mind the most was the fateful day that started it all. I wanted a niggers belongings so bad that I did the unthinkable to get it and it changed my entire world. I began to feel empty and confused. Just as I was about to faint away into la la land, my aunt knocks on the door.

"Mikey, someone named Rico is at the door for you."

I responded. "Thanks auntie, I'll get it."

I went to the door and there was Rico with long white paper in his hand that looked like blue prints. I step into the hallway and pull the door behind me so that my aunt is not privy to my business. He was quick as a motherfucker in getting me what I needed.

"This is everything you asked for and some. Yo. I even got their scheduled. Mike, I got to take care of something so here you go. Black, handle your business. I'll check you tomorrow. Same bat time, same bat channel."

Rico left and I re-entered the apartment. Locking the door behind me, I headed directly to my room. I closed the door and laid the paperwork on my bed and spread it out so that I could get an overall view. The page had four names on it. Fat Jack, Chad, Ronnie, and Lynn. I glanced through the pages, got out a pen, and started taking notes. I was looking at the arterial as if Machiavelli would look at it. I start applying the principles I learned from reading books on the art of war and strategy. I noticed Fat Jack never leaves his game room. He must be guarding something big in there. He sells weight from there, which means hitting at the right time will yield cash and drugs in abundance. Chad is a flamboyant old timer who can be seen on any given day strolling up and down 125th Street looking for attention and affirmation. That makes it much easier to get him. Ronnie is a young hustler who loves motorcycles and cars. He could be found in one or the other. Lynn was the tricky one. Although he never leaves his house. It makes him easy to be found. But a man in his own environment is dangerous. I called Rico after I came up with a workable plan. I tell him to meet me with all his boys at their spot in the morning.

CHAPTER THIRTEEN

I woke up early the next morning. This time it was not to look for a job, but to do a job. I hadn't spent any real time with my aunt since I'd been home. This move was going to allow me to really do her right. When I got outside in front of the building, it was so nice that I decided I was going to walk all the way uptown. I left my crib walking across all the avenues up 112th Street to Morningside Avenue. On the way there, I meet Detective Hartsfield. He was the arresting officer in my case and seemed to have a hard on for me now that I was much older and on the street. He pulled up along side me in a maroon classic Capri. He has one of those faces that you never forget. In a superficial inquisitive tone he says, "Hey Mikey, you found a job yet? You may have gotten older but you're the same ole little juvenile delinquent from a time not so long ago."

I am patiently listening to everything he has to say but letting it go in one ear and out the other. I sarcastically reply, "Are you finished, Detective?"

He rebuts with his own brand of sarcasm, "No, are you

finished, that is the question. I'm gonna say this one time Mr. Fraser. Don't come out thinking you are going to fuck up my streets cause I'll be watching you, you hear me!"

I keep my eyes fixed on him without responding. I start to walk away and detective Hartsfield yells another sarcastic insult.

"Michael. Keep your eyes on the prize." I suck my teeth and keep it moving to my destination. I had not time to hear what he was saying. After all, he was coming at me sideways. I reach the spot and everyone is there waiting for me. I have the set of altered blueprints that I got from Rico outlining the operation. I laid it across the table and began to explain it.

"What you have before you is the exact way this operation is to go down. In order for it to work successfully you'll have to execute it to the letter. Now based on these guys character traits I have designed a formula to get maximum results. I focused on their weakness rather than their strengths."

As I was describing the events, I could see all of them gesturing as if they are forming mental images of the way in which it will be carried out.

I continued. "This guy Fat Jack never leaves the game room, which means the stash is there also. Three of you will be responsible for locking him up in that game room. Take out all the phones and gag him: leave the rest to me.

This guy Chad is out in the public eye like Gotti or something. He feels protected around the people. He'll have to be taken in the open. There is no two ways about that. I prefer when he gets his morning coffee and hash browns from Copeland's. Why, because less people are there in the morning. Bring him directly to the spot and don't answer any questions. Put the child lock on the doors so he can't get out. In terms of Ronnie, I got plans for him. Rico, you can come with me to handle that. I want to make sure you understand me clearly. Don't take nothing form these niggers but the drugs and the money. I mean nothing else."

There were two meter man uniforms on the side of the floor. I suggested they use them in order to gain access behind fat jacks locked doors. I sent those gangster unit niggers to handle the fat jack thing. They all seemed to have a deeper bond that went far beyond that crew shit. The morning was still young but I wanted them to roll in time to catch all of them. So I sent them on their specific assignments. I had to make room for them possibly fucking up. After all, they didn't know me that well and I damn sure wasn't trusting them to be on point. No sooner than me and Rico get halfway to our destination he gets a call on his cell phone from Half a Dollar giving him the run down on what's going on inside Fat Jack's joint.

Apparently they got in without a hitch. His man Young God simply knocked on the door that separated the customers from himself and flashed a bogus I.D. once the door was opened it was obvious that letting him in was the wrong thing to do. Just as he suspects foul play, Young God pulls out a forty-five caliber with a silencer on it and shoots the doorman in the stomach. He goes down while Jack is looking on shitting bricks and begging for his life. Young god lets bank and half in. Fat Jack realizes he is at the end of the road and doesn't have a clue. Young God hits him with the butt of the gun and stakes his claim.

"Aight motherfucker, you know what this is. Don't start no shit, there won't be none."

Fat Jack is begging uncontrollably. "G god don't kill me, please don't kill me!"

Young God is not moved by his tears.

"Shut the fuck up. You wasn't crying when you was selling that ounce a minute ago." In a humble submissive tone Jack pleads, "Look, take the money, it's under the freezer, right there. Take it! It don't mean nothing to me. I got a daughter I want to see grow up."

Young God extends more humor, which adds insult to injury. "Then tell me where the work is and I think you'll live to see her graduate."

In a phony sense of shock, as if he doesn't know what he was talking about, Jack says, "What work?"

He fucked up when he did that. Young God was incensed. "Now that's the wrong answer! Try again."

Fat Jack is now bleeding from the mouth.

"Man, I'm telling you, the work is finished. I sold the last of it." Just as he completes his sentence bank finds the work. Bank is holding two large zip lock bags full of dope.

"Bingo! I found the jackpot."

Young is boiling. "You lied to me fat ass. You don't have any respect for me. What have I done to deserve this disrespect?" He looks at his boys to get some feedback as to what his next move is going to be. Half a Dollar gives his instructions.

"Tie his ass up and take him to the back. Make sure he's tied tight." Meanwhile he is ripping the phones out of the sockets. He yells for them to hurry up.

They lock Jack in the back and shut the gate down as they exit. They all jump in the car to head back to the drop off spot with what appears to be two kilos of heroine before picking up Chad. They are all in the car discussing the situation. Young God is happy as hell.

"I don't know about ya'll but these two bricks of dope we got is a lot to smile about. We got over a million dollars in our possession."

Half a Dollar adds his two cents, "Fuck that right now. I'm thinking about the stupid shit we just did."

Bank is looking at him as if he is crazy or something. "Did you hear what that man just said? We got over a million dollars in our possession. Don't nothing sound fucked up about that."

Young God turns to Half a Dollar. "Yeah nigger, you trippin right now. Open the window and catch your breath."

He hits right back trying to get them to understand the gist of what he was saying. "Trippin! I'm trippin, man. We just left a motherfucker alive that had over a million dollar worth of work. Fuck that, turn around."

Young God looks at him in shock.

"Nigger you stone cold crazy!" Half insists. "Turn around, yo. We are going to do this my way. I ain't leaving no boogie man around to haunt me later."

Bank looks at him. "Our instructions were to tie him up and leave him alive."

"Fuck those instructions, I'm not feeling taking no orders from no Johnny come on the spot. Turn the fuck around now!'

They reluctantly turn around and head back to the candy store. Half gets out.

"Give me the keys and stay right here. I'll be right out."

Young God hands him the keys. Half goes inside, shoots Jack twice in the head. He notices that Fat Jack still has his Rolex on. He takes it off his wrist and puts it in his pocket. He come back out and gets in the car. They drive off.

"Now was that hard, he asks?" Young God responds,

"Yeah, you damn right. Now we got a body that could have been taken care of by someone else."

Half is not concerned with his sentiments. "Yeah whatever. We got bodies anyway. One more aint gonna kill us."

Uptown in Parkchester, me, Rico and his man are in front of Ronnie's house. It is away from the hood in a quiet suburban environment. Ronnie is in the house with a bitch getting his dick sucked. We can see right through the window. He has on a robe and she is naked. The three of us are in the car waiting for the right moment to run up in there on his ass. Rico has binoculars and is getting a birds eye view of his crib.

"Damn that bitch can swallow a dick!"

His man snatches the binoculars from him. "Let me see. Now that's a fine looking asshole. Ugly niggers get all the good pussy when they got money."

I ask for the binoculars. "Let me see for a second. It's on. Now is a better time than ever to roll up in there. I hope we catch him busting a nut."

The three of us get out of the car and approach the house from the back. Instead of breaking any doors or anything, we use electronic scramblers to open the garage door and enter the house. Rico trips over an electrical cord making a little noise. I whisper, "Shhhh, you want to let him know we are here?"

We go upstairs and come down to the living room area

where Ronnie is freaking off. He is fucking her in the ass. I could hear her saying, “Ooh! Fuck me daddy. Cum inside me.”

While he is cumming we all walk into the living room. I am pointing the gun at Ronnie.

“ I hope it felt good to you.”

Ronnie reaches for his gun on the nightstand near him. Was he crazy?

“Now don’t you go making a bad decision worse, I said. Get your motherfucking hands up! You too bitch. Rico get his gun, he is not going to need it.”

Rico takes the gun from the nightstand. I signal for his man to put a set of handcuffs on Ronnie. Ronnie is trying to figure it all out.

“I don’t know what the fuck this is all about but if you disappear in five minutes I’ll forget this little incident ever happened.”

We all start to laugh at that shit. Rico had to add his smart ass remark.

“You can forget from now until Armageddon. Reality will help you jog your memory cause we aint going nowhere.”

Ronnie tries to reason with us at this point. “What the fuck do you want? Money? I’ll give you money. Ten thousand a piece?”

Rico makes it plain for him. “We don’t want money.

We want a cut from all your legitimate operations and we want to be plugged into your guinea friends."

That statement took me aback a little. I thought the plan was to get the money and get the fuck out of the game. It sounded to me like Rico had an agenda altogether different from what we discussed. Was that record label shit some type of scheme to get me to go along with his move? Ronnie knows that was not an option. It would mean certain death to him.

"Now you know I can't do that, that's like signing my own death certificate." I was more concerned about the money and the drugs, fuck that shit Rico was talking about. Nonetheless I had to roll with it because I didn't want to show dissent among us in front of Ronnie. I had a means to make him agree to our demands.

"Oh, you will do what he asked and I am going to give you just the right dosage of incentive to do it." I point the gun at his head. "Bend him over that table right there," I instructed.

I pulled a disposable camera out of my back pocket. I made Rico pull his pants down. Rico gets the picture of what is about to happen.

Ronnie is begging softly, "Don't do this to me man. My manhood is all I got."

"That's why I'm taking it. I am going to take a few snapshots of me running up in you. If you cooperate I will send you the negatives and that will be the end of it. No harm, no foul. If you don't, these pictures will hit every street corner where you do business. Everyone from here to Chicago will know that the man they respect is nothing more than a punk ass pillow biter."

As I penetrated Ronnie he begins to scream like a chicken in a slaughterhouse. I wanted to savor the moment. It was mostly personal for me. I just wanted to feel the brown on my dick once again. I signaled for Rico to come and get some. I knew he was thirsty as well. I also didn't want to be the only one feeding my appetite for a little delicious. We were fucking him like cockaholics. The bitch was stunned. She also looked turned on by it. I could see it in her eyes. I had to say focused though. I knew what I really came here for.

"I guess it's safe to ask where the money is now!"

"It's in my room, in a safe behind my bed."

"Well let's get to stepping," I insisted. He pulls up his pants and we leave the living room and head for the bedroom.

"What's the combo?" I asked.

Ronnie reluctantly replies, "Twenty-eight right, thirty six left, all the way around twice, then four right."

I enter the bedroom first to make sure he wasn't leading me up there to pull out a gun in the stash or some shit. Just like he said, the safe was right behind the door. I approached it and put my hands to work. Like magic the door opened for me.

"Bingo!!" I shouted. My eyes almost popped out of my head looking at all that cash.

"This is incentive enough for me to keep hush hush about these flicks."

"You got what you want, take it, it's yours."

"Oh, we plan to," Rico asserts. I looked at Rico and told him to bag that shit up so we could get the fuck out of there.

"Are you going to kill me?" Ronnie asks. I put his mind at ease.

"Fuck no! I need you alive. You think I just finished digging your guts out for nothing. I'm gonna pimp you like a ho on Broadway, or else."

"Or else what?!" Ronnie asks.

"Or else those pictures go out, that's what. Meanwhile, don't call us, we'll call you."

We exit the bedroom, Ronnie has the look of a woman who has just been beaten and humiliated by her man. He's too ashamed to utter a word to anyone. We go to the car and make our way back to the spot.

CHAPTER FOURTEEN

Unbeknownst to me, on the other side of town, Half and those gangster unit niggers had not only fucked things up, but apparently somebody left the gate up when I gave specific order to pull it down. I also found out it was Half. He left it open when he went back to kill him, another wrong move. Little kids thought the store was open and went in and found Jack and his man dead. The kids were banging on the glass.

"Fats, hurry up, I need four quarters." He notices the door inside the store is slightly ajar. "Fats, you in there?" He looked around sensing something was wrong. He goes in and finds both bodies sprawled across the floor with Fats head oozing white mass.

Shortly after the bodies were discovered, police are on the scene. The regular police get there first, then super cop gets there with his partner.

"What do you have?" Detective Hartsfield asks the detective on the scene.

"We have a Calvin Barnes, a.k.a. Fat Jack and a John

Doe, for the moment, laid out with bullets in their heads in the back of the joint. That's what you got."

Hartsfield wants to solve this in a hurry. "Any leads?" Sarcastically he replies, "A lead to nowhere. We got a clean bullet casing, probably wiped off before they got here and a store full of fingerprints. Problem is, this is a game room and a candy store. People buy candy and play game in here. We also got a couple of kids who say they haven't seen shit. I think that narrows it down to about a billion suspects in the naked city."

That seems like an unacceptable answer to Hartsfield. "Where are the kids now?" asks Hartsfield.

The detective points to a group of kids standing on the sidewalk and says, "Over there." Hartsfield puts on his best Sherlock Holmes face and walks over to the kids.

"Alright, which one of you wants to make a crisp ten dollar bill?" The first kid that answered was obviously the baddest ass out of the group.

"It all depends." One kid answered. "What we gotta do for it. No snitches over here, if that's what you mean." He didn't know it but that was the response Hartsfield needed to reel him in.

"Then you must know something. You can't snitch if you don't know nothing."

The second kid gives his smart retort, "Well technically, we don't know nothing."

He is no match for Hartsfield's wit. "Well not so technically, what do you know?" asks Hartsfield. The first kid signals to the second kid.

"Shut up, you talk too much."

Hartsfield is now getting vexed. "I don't have time for games. I'll take all of your little asses downtown and make your mammas get out of bed to come get you. Now take this ten and gimme what I need."

That was enough for the kids. "When we got here earlier, a guy was in front of the store giving us money to come back later."

Hartsfield knows he is getting somewhere now. "Do you remember what he looked like?"

The young man holds his hand to his head as if trying to recall the man's face.

"He was dark skinned with a scar on his mouth. We asked him about it and he said he was shot in the mouth. We thought that was cool as shit."

"Is that it?" Hartsfield asks.

"Yeah, that's it. Oh yeah, he talked funny too. Ok Mr. Detective, you got twenty dollars worth of information for ten dollars."

"Sue me." Hartsfield replies. He begins to walk off and he takes a couple of steps, the kids grab onto his jacket.

"Detective!" one of them shouts.

"Yeah kid." He offers some more information in hopes

of retrieving his bounty.

"One other thing. I noticed that Fats didn't have his watch on when I found him. He never took that watch off. They must have took it."

Hartsfield begins to salivate. "What, was it a special kind of watch?"

"Hell yeah!" he responds. "It was a Rolex loaded with diamonds."

Hartsfield was satisfied with what he got from them. He goes into his pocket and pulls out a twenty-dollar bill and hands it to the kid.

"You see, it pays to snitch sometimes." He gets into his car with his partner and drives off.

Meanwhile, me, Rico and the rest of his clan are back at the spot. Half and his clique are already at the table when we get there. Money and dope is on the table. We come in with our spoils and add them to the spoils. Everybody sits but me. Because I orchestrated the whole thing, most at the table see me as a hero and leader, like I knew they would.

"Behold, this is your key to liberation. This is your way out. As long as you keep it real with each other, you will always have it. In America, it's a fight for peace, freedom and money. We have made war, so that we may have peace. Enjoy my niggers, enjoy!"

They all go crazy at the table. I feel like Hitler giving a

speech to his Nazi regime. They all start playing with the money, lighting cigars, popping Moet and sniffing some of the dope. I pull Bank to the side to discuss how everything went at Fat Jacks.

"Main man, let me talk to you for a second." We both go into the back room. He is looking suspicious as to why I singled him out.

"What's up?" he asks. I get straight to the point.

"Everything went down alright. Did you make sure you clipped the wires?"

"It went somewhat kosher."

I am puzzled. I know what that means.

"Half killed them," he blurted.

"He did what?!" trying not to take in what he just said.

"I wasn't about to argue with a nut with a loaded gun. He goes postal when he don't get what he wants. Anyway, we should have never taken Half on this one. Killing people is his passion."

I knew it was over. Something always goes wrong when you add anyone other than yourself.

"Now we all going down because a motherfucker don't listen. I told you from the jump that if you listen to what I say nobody would get dead and we would all get what we wanted, but there's a Jesse James in every bunch!"

"It might ease your mind to know that no one saw us."

I look in amazement. I realize that what could go

wrong, did. I'm not really that worried though because my primary goal was to obtain financial resources to look out for my aunt, and if at all possible, to be out of here.

I look at Bank. "I'll make it right, it's not your fault." We go back into the room where everybody is dividing up the spoils. I look at everyone and put on a face of happiness as to keep everyone off guard.

"Where's my share?" I ask. "Bag my cut so I can start living." Rico pushes about seven stacks of hundred dollar bills toward me. I place it in a knapsack.

Rico looks at me and says, "You the man right now baby. I knew you could make it happen, and with Ronnie under the arm pits we got more of this coming in."

I was out and didn't want to hear anything at the moment. All I wanted to do was get back to my aunt and map out a plan for her happiness.

"I got some shit to take care of. I'm out. I'll get with you later. Another day, another way." I walk out the door and head for my house. I knew as soon as I walked out that Half would be curious as to what me and Bank were talking about. He started inquiring as soon as I left.

"What did he want to talk to you about?" Half asks Bank. Bank knew what was up.

"Oh nothing big, I told him everything went down smooth and not to worry."

"And what did he say when you told him?" Half asked.

"That everything would be alright." Bank was twisting my words so he wouldn't cause conflict. Half ponders over what Bank told him as if he had something up his sleeve.

On the way home, I see none other than my favorite detective. I think he has ESP or something.

"Hey, Mr. Fraser, it's me again. It thought you might want to know, somebody just knocked off a fixture in your old hood."

"Why would I want to know that?" I asked.

"Because when shit falls, it falls hard. And you know what? The wrong person ends up stinking. I'm still watching you, and believe you me, if I watch a little longer I'm going to get the answers." He drives off. He and his partner are talking as they drive away.

"You ever thought for once that he might not be thinking about any wrongdoing?" he asks Hartsfield.

"Please, he got the mark of the beast now. One you get that first felony, society says it's over, and they respond by committing more crimes. I'd say he was ripened for another murder. Five says he's guilty as sin and I'm going to prove it."

"The bet is sealed, you're on."

I get back to this house to find my sister babysitting my cousin.

"Auntie just called and asked me if you were here. I told her

I didn't see you since I got here," my sister asserts.

"Did she say what she wanted?"

"No, she just wanted to speak to you I guess." She was on her way into my aunt's bedroom when I stopped her in her tracks.

"Wait, I have something I want to speak to you about. But first you have to promise me two things."

She looks at me crazy, "What?"

"I need your word first."

"Yes, you have my word, but if you weren't my brother I would never think about promising or giving my oath blindly."

I spit it out, "I came across a few dollars and I don't want Auntie to know, but I want you to look after her with it. It's not a million dollars or nothing like that but it's enough for her to make it for a good while." I open the bag to show her the contents.

"That's more than a few dollars. Where did you get this money? Mike, tell me you're not on your way back to jail. Did you kill somebody?" I put her mind at ease, even if I wasn't sure what was going to become of me.

"No, I haven't killed anybody since I been home. Just promise me that whatever happens you'll take care of Auntie for me, you can even give mamma some. Now put this in the room." I hand her the bag.

I had to go downstairs to catch some air. I knew if I

wanted to get away with this thing I would have to do something that would land me in jail for the rest of my days. I had to get rid of Half because he was a loose cannon and a thorn in my side. If he got caught, the whole shit would be blown and we would all get an accessory to murder for his dumb ass move.

Half and the rest of them are still at the spot. He is fucked up as hell and begins talking off the wall. They are all still there celebrating. In his drunk stupor, he addresses Rico, Young God, Bank and the rest of them.

"Your boy was too good to party with us. That motherfucking fly by night think he can just be in just like that, take our loot? Hell that's my mother fucking loot, I do all the killing around this motherfucker."

"You roasted man, go home and get some sleep," Rico demands.

"Fuck sleep! I'm gonna sleep when I damn well feel like it."

Rico ordered someone to get Half some milk. Half was not finished with his tirade. "You niggers always undermining everybody. Especially you Rico. We didn't really need your man. I think it's time I assumed my position on this ship. I should be the captain."

Rico sarcastically concedes. "That's what you want, then you can have it. I'm not trying to be no captain. Everybody is equal. Nobody else is complaining about the decision to bring Mike in."

Bank tries to break the ice. "Ya'll know he don't mean none of that shit. He's just tore up that's all." Bank looks at Half. "Come on baby boy, let's go for a walk. I'll take you to the corner store to get you some coffee and milk." Half and Bank leave for the store. Young God and Rico are holding a sidebar about what just went down. Rico is eager to say what is on his mind. "That nigger is a loose cannon. He's gonna get all our asses knocked."

Young God makes light of Half's tirade. "Ain't nobody getting knocked. By tomorrow he's not even going to remember a word he said."

Rico is not convinced. "Keep believing that. He already showed us it's all about him. He's ego trippin'. They say that when a man is drunk he is always telling the truth. He's telling us exactly how he feels. The sooner we realize that the better."

"We'll just wait until he comes down off his high and take it from there. Give him the benefit of the doubt. Now, I want to finish partying. He holds up some of the money in his hand. We got more to be happy about than sad."

Half and Bank are in the store across the street. He is trying to sober Half up with no doze, coffee and milk. He is dragging him around the store. Bank grabs some additional items and heads for the counter. He motions to Half. "Here lean on this." Half leans on the ice freezer with his hands stretched over it. Detective Hartsfield is on his way in the store to get coffee. He greets the cashier.

"Hey Arty. Business slow tonight?"

Arty responds. "Not since you walked in. How's the misses?

She throw you out yet?"

"No, not yet." He walks to the counter to pay for the donut and coffee. Half is still leaning over the icebox. Hartsfield notices the watch on half's wrist. He inquires because he knows it is not everyday that a man wears a watch like that.

"Nice watch. You struck the lottery? Where'd you buy it? I want to own one just like it someday.

Half is oblivious. You can tell by his response.

"Your mother bought it for me!"

Bank knows he is in deep shit. He also didn't realize that Half had on Fat Jack's watch. All of the excitement about the money made all of them blind.

"You'll have to excuse him. He's a little tipsy that's all."

"You can say that again. Let's see if downtown can take him off his toes and put him on his feet." Hartsfield signals for his partner to come in to assist. Bank tries to squash what he knows will be bad for him and the others if Half has to go downtown.

"There's no need for that officer. I can get in a cab with him and see to it that he gets in his house."

Hartsfield is not amused. "I bet you can, but just to be on the safe side, I think I better take him in. I couldn't live with myself if he stumbles and busts his head or something." Hartsfield proceeds to handcuff Half.

They take him downtown and charge him with public drunkenness as a legal means to hold him in custody. Bank goes back to the spot to let everyone know that Half has just been arrested. He's out of breath from running from the store to the spot. He knocks on the door, Rico answers and opens the door.

"They got Half!" Rico doesn't know how to respond.

"Who got Half?" everybody is roused and listening intently.

"Five-O got Half. When we was in the store he was acting up and a knocker came in. He took him downtown. He was asking about a watch Half had on. I think he took the shit from Jack. I didn't even notice it. We got to get Half out of there before they find out about the watch."

Rico is trying to maintain his composure. "Calm down motherfucker, first things first. What watch? I know damn well you ain't talking about Fat Jack's watch?"

Rico grabs him and throws him against the wall. They know they have to get down to the precinct before this nigger starts acting like a parrot.

At the police station, Half is slowly coming out of his stupor. Hartsfield is digging for a breakthrough in his case by bombarding Half with tons of questions.

"Talk to me you murdering son of a bitch. Give me what I need to know and you can go in that cell and sleep all day if you like. I've seen your kind before. I've been on the job a long time."

Half responds, no sure of what he is really saying. "All I know is I didn't kill anybody."

That's what Hartsfield loves to hear.

"Go right ahead, open up the door. What are you implying? You know who did?"

"I ain't said that, but your boy, good old Mr. Fraser might know something." He doesn't know it but he is getting just the rise out of Hartsfield he has been craving for. This is a chance of a lifetime to get Michael Fraser for good.

"You mean Michael Fraser?" Half leads him into it. He is obviously getting sober by the minute.

"You said it, I didn't. Anyway, you do the math. I heard he already got a murder charge for sticking up somebody. It is a funny coincidence that as soon as he gets home shit starts around here; at least that's what I hear. I ain't from around here so I don't know everything."

Hartsfield is thirsty now. "Come on son, work with me. You got the watch, you gonna have to come up with a little more than that." As Hartsfield finishes his sentence Half sees Rico and Young God entering the precinct.

"Oh shit! Half's outburst makes Hartsfield turn

around. Just as he does, the desk officer points to him to direct Rico and Young God to his desk. Half is rattled.

"Look, I didn't tell you anything!"

Hartsfield doesn't want him to punk out on him. He's too close to getting his man. "Hold tight. Keep your panties on."

Rico and Young God reach Hartsfield's desk and look at Half in a suspicious manner. Hartsfield wants to know why they feel they owe him a visit.

"How may I help you boys?"

Rico, with a look of disdain, says, "You can help us by letting us know if you charging our boy with anything so we can meet you at the courthouse with bail."

Hartsfield sees things slipping away from him by the minute. "Now, now, now, don't go sending your boy downtown in front of a judge before his time. You'll all have a turn at that."

Young God gets mad. "And what the fuck is that supposed to mean?"

In a smooth tone Hartsfield delivers his response. "I'm just callin' it like I see it, but anyway, that's a story of its own. I'm not going to hold him, I think he's sobered up rather nicely. As for your future convictions, I suggest you stay the fuck away from Mr. Fraser."

Rico is not trying to hear the rhetoric. "Is he free to go or what?"

"Yeah, he's free to go, as free as a bird in the sky."

Young God had to get a dig in. "Thank you overseer, I mean officer." They head for the door, but before they get there Hartsfield calls out to Half. They all turn around.

Hartsfield winks at him as a bitch would wink at a man and says, "Thanks for everything." They all turn back around and exit the precinct. Bank is already inside the car. Half is in the middle in the backseat. Rico is in the front and Young God gets in the back with Half and Bank.

"Seems like you was having a pretty good conversation. I almost didn't want to interrupt."

Half tries to act mad to cloak his deceit. "Fuck you. What I look like, a snitch to you? Who the fuck am I going to snitch on, myself?"

Rico shoots right back, "You said it, I didn't." Half notices they are driving towards the water. Just as he realizes it, Rico puts the automatic lock on the doors.

Half wants answers, "Why are we going this way? I know we not going to pick up no work with all of us in here!"

Rico looks at Young God, smiling slightly, "Ain't nobody picking up nothing. We going to drop something off."

"Is there work in the car?"

"Ain't no work," Rico responds. "No work in this ride but this joint is definitely dirty as a motherfucker," Rico says, referring to his suspicion that Half snitched.

Realizing what was happening Half gets frantic.

"I know y'all don't think I told. Oh shit, it's like that? That's how ya'll motherfuckers going out?" Half reached for the door.

There is a police car behind them. Rico spotted it from his rear view mirror. He calmly looks back at Bank and Young God.

"Five-O right behind us." Rico turns on the music and cracks the window slightly and tells everyone to make movements to the rhythm of the beat.

"Just start singing and clapping to the song." The cops move to the side of the car while the light is still on red. Half is trying to get some line of communication to the cops but the sound of the music drowns him out. The police officer looks at Rico and gives him a sign to turn the music down some and drives off.

The cop in the passenger seat looks at the cop driving and says, "That car was too noisy for them to be guilty of doing anything. You can hear them coming a mile away."

Rico gives the officer a thumbs up. When they get far ahead of him he shows it with an expression of relief. They reach the Westside Highway, right by the water. They all get out of the car. Rico reaches under the seat and recovers his 45 caliber. Half, realizing this is his last chance to save his life, pleads one last time.

"Yo, Bank, you my nigger. You going to let these niggers fade me?" Bank knows his hands are tied and has no problem letting him know it.

"I wash my hands of it. You're out of control now You don't listen to nobody!"

Rico wants him to know the real deal. "Nobody is going to fade you. You gonna fade yourself. I'm gonna give you a chance to run like hell."

Half knows there is a catch. "Then what?"

"Then nothing."

"If you was going to let me run, why you brought me over here then?"

"Because this is your track." He lifts his hands towards the Hudson River. "You can either sink or swim. At least you have a chance at life."

Half looks at the water and realizes his fate. "Alright then, if this is how it's got to be."

He grabs Bank and interlocks his hands under his arms and falls backwards into the river. "We'll see you in hell nigger."

Rico tries to grab Bank but he is unsuccessful. Bank manages to hold onto a log at the base of the dock. The undercurrent is dragging Half under and he is trying to hold onto Bank, pulling him off the log. Bank is crying for help.

"Somebody help me! Please help me!"

Rico sees a long piece of railing pipe about six feet away. He grabs it and puts it in the water to try to save Bank. His attempts are futile and Bank slips away into the blackness of the current.

CHAPTER FIFTEEN

Seven months had passed and I was spending money like crazy. Those two detectives were on my ass, following me around and shit; I couldn't breathe. Diane hit me with some new that brought tears of joy to my eyes. She was pregnant and due at the end of the year. Life was really looking up in spite of all the shit I was dealing with. Rico and Young God were still gambling by staying in the game. I backed off from both of them and decided I was going to count my blessings and make good on the paper I had. Me and Diane decided we were going to invest in property in Baltimore, Maryland and raise our child. I was on my way to achieving the American dream without the help of the system.

Everything was good for me, with the exception of my health. I was feeling sluggish all the time and I was losing a lot of weight. My eyes started to sink in and my mouth would be dry all the time. Everyone was telling me to go to the doctor but I was not trying to hear that. Besides, I had no time for bad news, I was trying to do things. I was pretty confident that Hartsfield would meet a dead end in terms of trying to pin anything on me. Rico and Young God covered most of the tracks and I had no reason to believe either of them would rat me out. I was banking on the fact that they were going to be murdered in the game before they could get a chance to say anything.

I was hanging out with the two homos from the salon, Precious and Toni on a regular basis. I would sneak with them over the bridge to the Quarry. It was located over the 135th Street Bridge. I would simply come in as if I was looking for Toni or Precious. The bouncers would let me come in to look for them and I would never come out. The atmosphere was always loose and crazy but nonetheless there was a hold on me to keep coming back. In the bathrooms would be men engaging in all types of fucking and sucking. Men were in stalls abusing themselves and baby dykes could be seen fondling each other. Men would be face fucking each other and tag team fucking like Batman and Robin.

Behind the DJ booth would be men chain fucking each other while others were have cum drinking contests. There were also other weird contest going on all around the joint. It was weird, but no less interesting. There were pearl necklace contests and commitment ceremonies. They also had mini parties in selected areas of the club for what they called, new converts. These were guys and girls who were coming out of the closet. Precious and Toni always introduced me as a friend of Dorothy. It meant that I wasn't a homo but I was accepting of the gay lifestyle. This was to ensure that my integrity was maintained on the street. I told them that if I was going to be hanging out with them, the last thing I wanted was some fag coming up to me on the street putting me on broad street in front of everyone.

I also had my girl's feelings to protect, not to mention I was about to be a father. There was something about being a father that brought new life to me. I knew that this was a way in which I could start life over through my little man's life. He was to be the hope that was lost in my life, at least that's what I thought.

I got a call from Diane the night before she was to go for her monthly check up. She was bleeding from her nose and wanted to go to the hospital. She told me to meet her at Harlem Hospital in the emergency room. I didn't know what to think. Was my baby alright? When I got there doctors were poking her in her arm and taking blood. Her blood pressure was low and they said she was possibly going into pre-mature labor. There were other doctors talking on the side as if something else was wrong. I wanted some answers and I wanted them fast. As they ushered her upstairs to the delivery room, I was called by one of the attending doctors into a small cubicle. I was asked to have a seat. As I sat down I could feel sorrow in the air. I just knew something was so wrong that nothing or no one could make it right. The doctor, in a voice that was sullen and weak, told me of the problem.

"Mr. Fraser, you're the father of this child, correct?"

"Yes I am." He opened the chart in front of him and began to go into detail.

"I am sorry but I have some bad news concerning your child and his mother. I don't know how we did not pick it up before but it seems that your fiancé is suffering from an advanced stage of HIV and there is a strong possibility that your child is infected as well. We didn't want to tell her in her present condition, considering she is due to deliver prematurely. The illness has caused her immune system to shut itself down, leaving her and the child open to various infections. Her chronic bleeding is a result of an attack on her blood cells. The disease is causing the body to fight against itself. You or she will have to make a choice as to what should be done if we can't save the baby. Chances are she will lose so much blood during delivery that we will have to make a sacrifice. It is up to the both of you. I thought it should be you. I thought it should be you to tell her. We don't have much time so you will have to act fast. We would also need you to give a blood sample as well."

If there ever was a time I felt like the world was coming to an end it was now. What in the world did I do to deserve this? More importantly, what did Diane or my child do to deserve this? How could I tell the mother of my child that she was suffering from an illness that would mean her untimely demise and that she might die trying to deliver the baby. I also had to think about the fact that she was HIV positive. But how could that be? Just as fast as I uttered the words my heart gave up the answer. I had given her a virus that I didn't even know I had. I got it from Dee Dee. It all started to make sense. I was feeling sick and sluggish because my body was telling me something, telling me something I didn't want to hear. Dee Dee had managed to get the last laugh after all and he even managed to make my kid and girl feel it.

The doctor didn't have to make the call, I knew what I had to do. I went upstairs to the delivery room and faced my demons. I had no choice but to tell her. As she lay on the table in pain I had knew I still had to tell her, no matter how painful. The contractions were less than two minutes apart and the doctors feared the worst. When I looked in her eyes, I knew I could not summon the strength to tell her. I ran outside the delivery room as the tears began to roll down my face. For the first time in my life I felt love and compassion for someone other than a family member. She was the mother of my child. The doctor was making his way into the delivery room when I stopped him.

"Doc, can I talk to you for a second?"

"Sure, but make it quick, they just called me from

downstairs to tell me that she ready to have the baby. Did you talk to her yet?"

"No, I haven't. But I have decided to make the decision for her. I love her dearly, and I love my first born more than you will ever know. I can have another child but there will only be one Diane. I want you to save her, Doc. At all costs save her! I'll sign whatever I have to sign."

The doctor looked at me as if he not only knew that was the right choice but that he hoped I would make that choice. I knew if I told her she would have preferred to die and save her child. I had ruined this woman's life. The least I could do was to let her enjoy whatever life she had left. As each minute passed I could hear the screams of labor intensifying. I couldn't go in because that meant I would have to look her in the face and conceal my deceit. After eight exhausting hours the doctor came out of the delivery room with his head hung down. His face had the look of death.

"Mr. Fraser, I'm sorry but we couldn't save the baby." I kinda figured that. I was expecting a miracle but I could live with it.

"I am afraid I have bad news. We weren't able to save your fiancé either. There was just too much blood loss. The baby wrapped itself in the umbilical cord which made it difficult to control the bleeding and get him out before he suffocated."

I didn't have the words to reply. I went into the room with the weight of the world on my shoulders. Both lifeless bodies were on that slab as if the world had left them for dead. It was a boy, and he looked just like his father. I decided he deserved a name. After all, he deserved a name and a funeral. I named him Michael Jr.

Diane's eyes were wide open, it was as if I could see right through her soul. She had the look of disappointment, as if I had let her down by not being in the room when she took her last breath. I let her down in more ways than one. She died not knowing the truth. She also died for no reason other than my stupidity.

All of a sudden I couldn't bare the thought of living anymore. There was no way I could face her family at a funeral. I looked upon her face and the face of my child one last time before I left the delivery room. I was going to walk out of there with a new look on life and a new way of sharing it. I was going to be honest with myself and others. I had deceived one person, I wasn't going to do it again. I made up my mind, I was going to check with my parole officer. He was looking for me for violating my curfew. I was going to finish the last thirteen months I owed the system and come out a new man. By then, everything with her parents would have subsided. Being at the funeral would only make it worse. I was going to finish my time and head for Baltimore. I was keeping the dream alive for both of us. I was also going to be honest about who I was. I called Precious and Toni and told them I was going in the morning. I made them an offer to wait for me until I got out and we could all make a move together to Baltimore and open a unisex salon of our own.

I was coming out of the closet. I was tired of lying. I was on the countdown to a new life, free from deceit and lies. If Dee Dee didn't do anything for me, she sure brought me out. Funny how things work themselves out.

I am sorry I had to lose two people to find that out. I am saying goodbye to Michael and hello to Michelle. See ya'll in Baltimore!

Homo Thug

Part 2

By

Asante Kahari

Published by

Harlem Book Center, Inc.
129 West 137th Street, 1B
New York, NY 10030
Tel: +1/646-739-6429

Warning!
This is work of fiction. All the characters, incidents and dialogues are the products of the author's imagination and are not to be construed as real. Any references or similarities to actual events, entities, real people, living or dead, or to real locales are intended to give the novel a sense of reality. Any similarity in other names, characters, entities, places and incidents is purely coincidental.

ISBN:978-0-9800822-0-3

AUTHOR'S ACKNOWLEDGEMENTS

This will not take very long. I want to thank Sidi, the publisher, for being ever so patient with me. (Asante kahari-NYS ID 85807350804 @690Gates Ave.Apt 5F,NY,NY11221, asantekahari@verizon.net 347-351-7343,home 718-443-0011).To Carmen Garrett, when my wife and I needed you the most you were always there. To Bernadette Jackson and Omar. Omar, your wife is a weirdo, just kidding, her MSW degree has blurred her vision. She is too damn idealistic. To Paulette, Nitivia, and Jaquasia, you are the worst neighbors in the world. Paulette Clemmons, you are not the next American Idol. Slow your role Grandma. T.D and LaShae Green, you guys are the best, well at least T.D. is. Your Wife is crazy. To the Jackson family, I know you don't like me but for the sake of your daughter you tolerate me. Uncle John, I love you dearly. To my Little Brother Danyule, I am amazed at what a man you have become. I love you very much, even when I can't show it. To my brother Troy and nephew Idris Mitchell, I know the power of love; you don't have to tell me, I feel it. Bilal and Sharon Carter. My sisters Jillian, Natosha, and Shanel, I would give a right arm to show you how much you truly mean to me. Kevin, there is a special bond I share with you that can't be explained. I worry about you even in my dreams. Jr, you are my brother. You can't choose your siblings, I wish I could. Akmir Grey, Otis Williams, Don Miller and Barbara, AKA Busy B. You have been more than a mother to me. Bobby and Tommy, love you dearly. I miss Gloria, Uncle William and Aunt Louise everyday. Shatae, Joyce and Tianna. Joyce we have been down this road before. I love you more than the world has water. Renee, Bobby, Michael, Ebony,Jamal, family is family. I have far too many uncles and aunts to name. Uncle Kenny, Trish, and Nate. The rest of you can charge it to my head. Don's wife Mel, Yaz, Whip, Diamond, China, DeNita, Steve Hall, Jeffrey Sledge, Diane Lee, I can't be sorry enough for the wrong I have committed against you, I am still paying for it. Nikki Jones and Family. Octavia Kahari, love you. Last but not least, to my wife, Olivia. I don't know where I would be had it not been for you. I still wonder why you keep on believing, keep on loving, keep on sharing. I know the love of God because I see it in your face every morning. If I forgot you it was probably intentional. Just because you are someone's friend doesn't necessarily mean that view you as the same. I am learning that slowly but surely.

Homo Thug

Part 2

By

Asante Kahari

PROLOGUE

I stand in shock with ringing ears and a heavy heart after the doctor tells me that both Dianne and my child are both in danger.

"The effects of the advanced form of HIV on her body means she is not strong enough to survive having the child," he says. "Either you or her have to decide which one of them to save."

I stand frozen by my paradox. The absurdity of power bestowed upon me by this doctor over the love of my life's life and/or my child's life has my head spinning. Or, is it that the walls are spinning and I'm the one that's standing still?

"You're running out of time," the doctor says. "You have to tell her right away about the HIV and the baby so she can make up her mind. We have to hurry up and get in there to try to save one of them."

I nod my understanding to his words and start making what is by far the longest walk of my life thus far.

***

Dianne looks like a weakened, feeble shell of herself when I slumber into her room. Yet, despite her deplorable condition, her eyes light up at the sight of me. Unfortunately, my eyes don't return the sparkle.

As only a woman can, my woman reads my mood and writes it with words as if she's placing it on the wall.

"What's wrong, Michael?" she asks. "Be straight with me no matter what. I've always told you that and up to now you've always listened."

"Foolish child," I think.

In reality, Dianne wishes I were real with her at all times like she thinks. Truthfully, I've been as plastic and fake as any one man could be to a woman. Now all of my chickens are coming home to roost.

"You have to sit down, Sweetie," I say. I don't know what else to say so why not?

"Michael, I'm in the damned hospital lying in a bed about to push out damned baby out if you don't keep stalling," she says. "Spit it out. Spit it the fuck out so I can push this baby out."

I can tell that the labor pains are getting the best of her. Poor Dianne, if only that were her only worry.

"We have to decide if you're going to try again with me for procreation or if the baby and I are going to do it on our own," I say out the side of my mouth.

"Michael, what the fuck?" Dianne yells. "I hate it when you get like this. Just tell me. Spit it out, man!"

I love my baby's strength. I love her feistiness. Heaven smiled upon me when she was sent my way. Of course like any other doggish-ass man I turned around and gave heaven my ass to kiss.

"Baby please just listens," I say. "The doctor says we're running out of time. Due to complications with your pregnancy he says you're not strong enough for both you and the baby to survive childbirth. He wants to know whether to commence efforts to save you or the baby."

"My baby or me," she says almost as if she's talking to herself. "Are you serious? What kind of complications?" I probably could have gotten away with shrugging away the question but like the shamefaced person that I am, guilt was written all over my face.

"What kind of complications?" she asks triggering no response from me. "Michael! What kind of fucking complications?"

"HIV," I whisper.

"Speak up," she demands. Again I whisper. "Michael! Spit it the fuck out!"

"Sweetie, you have an advanced stage of HIV but don't

worry it will all be alright," I say, running game. I know for a fact my game has run out.

"HIV? You didn't say HIV did you, Michael? How in the fuck can I end up with HIV?"

I have no words for my fiancee. All I have is a look of shame to present to the love of my life. She has much more to give to me.

Like Jesus pressed Olive Oil onto Dianne's head himself, her frail body all of a sudden becomes invigorated. She jumps out the bed and removes at the probes that are attached to her to monitor her in one powerful swipe of her hand.

Lunging at me like she's the stealthiest of Cheetahs that you'd see on Animal Planet, Dianne has me gripped up in an instant.

I feel like the room has gone totally black as she slams my head against the wall then on the tiled floors after I slump down to the ground.

"Baby, I'm sorry," I muster up the strength to say.

"You're goddamned right that you're sorry," Dianne screams. "How could you do this to me? I never fucking questioned you. You never heard about any of my doubts. You're a fucking peanut butter booty-ass nigga! You played me like that for real? You really, really did this to me?"

I'm not sure which is hurting me more, Dianne's words

or her slamming my head into the floor.

Feebly, I yell out her name. "Dianne… Dianne."

Yet, I'm certain that my voice is so weak that she can't even hear me.

If I said the room was turning black minutes ago by now it's pitched black. Just as I'm about to pass out I can only imagine that an orderly has come into the room since now I hear it loudly.

"Dianne… Dianne… Dianne."

Then there's a huge banging, a flicker of light amidst all of the darkness, and the sound of another name.

"Michael… Michael… Michael…"

I jump up to find my face drenched with sweat, my heart racing, my eyes bloodshot red, and excitement in the air.

Yet, as I come down from whatever high I was on or come back from whatever place I went to, I note that Dianne is no longer with me. My head is no longer being pounded against the floor. And my body is no longer in the hospital. The reality of my situation is ratified by the bars that are encaging me, the beast that's on the outside of the bars guarding, and the flashlight that the beast is holding in steady on me to the point that it's blinding me.

"I ain't gon' tell your ass one more time to stop it," the C.O. says.

I'm so fucked up right now that I don't even know which one of those bastards that it is.

After the C.O. walks away and after my heartbeat calms back down to a more acceptable pace, I remember where I am and what I'm doing.

For six months I've been serving out my sentence for violating my parole. I thought that time would heal all wounds but in my case I can't say that has been the case.

I still receive hate mail from Dianne's family. With each letter there's a promise of one new method of humiliating me that is of course more drastic than the last.

Secrets that I vowed to take with me to my grave they threaten to expose.

Of course they can't prove that I have HIV Based on the privacy of medical records the doctor couldn't divulge the true reason behind Dianne's untimely death.

All her people have on me is reflections and innuendos. They can't really prove shit.

But, everyone knows that the hood is the hood. You don't need shit to be tried and proven true. The rumor mill is the claimant, prosecutor, judge, and jury. Your rep is all you have and once your rep gets fucked up your entire life is fucked up.

One thing that the nightmares that I can't shake have done for me is caused me to change my mind about coming clean and changing my name from Michael to Michelle. Dianne's anger is obvious and authenticates the fact that she didn't deserve what she got. I was at fault not her. How in the hell could I run away like nothing happened with this ghost haunting the innermost corners of my psyche?

***

One month to go before I get out of here and I feel a little better mentally. I don't get letters anymore. After the couple letters I received to say that the propaganda campaign I put Precious and Toni on was bullshit her family pretty much left me alone.

As far as I'm concerned no news is good news. Maybe they don't totally believe the lies that Precious and Toni told for me in Dianne's family's presence but at least they are not still one-hundred-percent certain that I had something to do with my fiancee's death.

Growing up in the hood and living there all my life has taught me that it doesn't matter what people think about you as long as they ain't putting your name up in their mouth.

I'm thankful for small victories. Hell, I'm thankful for any type of victories I can get.

***

With my last night in jail I promise myself that I am crying my last tear, experiencing my last nightmare, and waking up in a cold sweat for the last time.

I have to find a way to funnel my thoughts in such a way that I am not tearing myself down all the time. I need to find a way to build myself up.

I think about reading some stuff on the internet about the Bloods and the Crips. Although I don't agree with gang violence at this point in my life, there's something to say about having someone else's back because he or she had yours, or in this case, paying someone back for taking your loved one out of the game.

Pay back is a motherfucker.

Right now, pay back is the only thing that's keeping me sane.

I stretch my mind as far as it can go and wrap myself around the tenets of settling scores.

"You can't just accept any bullshit," I tell myself. "Anybody anywhere will do any and everything that they want to do to you if they find out they can test you without absolution."

But, knowing that I'm about to be released from prison with no further restrictions on my ability to roam free tells me that I don't want to go too far in whatever plan I come up with.

I can't land myself back in prison. Whatever the future holds for me, I promise myself that it won't have anything at all to do with prison.

Suddenly I think back to Dee-Dee and how callous he/she was in getting the last laugh.

Not only was my life fucked up forever but my fiancee and unborn child were destined to die because of me.

No. It wasn't because of me. It was because Dee-Dee made some decision for me that I had no power to override.

My life was taken into Dee-Dee's hands and because of that my future wife and child had their lives taken into his hands as well.

"You have to be some sick, slimy fuck to even think of some foul shit like that," I tell myself.

But, as I'm talking to myself and becoming riled up I'm also salivating at the thought of exercising all of that power.

At many times in my life when I felt like I've been in control the system has always knocked me back down to size and shown me that I'm not really in control. I'm just a pawn on a fucking Chess board and I have no way in hell to get to the other side to promote myself.

As fucked up as Dee-Dee was I imagined how he must have felt knowing what my fate would be, what my fiancee's fate would be, what my unborn child's fate would be.

Dee-Dee was Hitler without a country to run and without any threat of other leaders trying to run him out of a country.

Day by day, I've found myself becoming drunk at the thought of that power. Just as in the days when Kurtis Blow was rapping "Yes, Yes, Y'all" I found myself having "If I ruled the world" moments.

I wasn't Shaka Zulu but my destiny was power- power over myself and power over everyone around me. Matter fact, I knew that I would have power over anybody that ever crossed my path.

***

So now that I know that the thought of power gets my dick harder than the sexiest chick and makes my blood boil hotter than the most violent volcano, I had to come up with the exact mission or cause to live by.

Yes, I would be the perpetrator but who would be my victims?

I feel myself being stuck inside the Candyman movie and exhorting someone to be my victim.

Who would the assholes be that I got to say my name

just one to many times?

Did it matter to me or should everyone be fair game?

I think about the anger I feel each time one of my fellow inmates receives baby pictures.

I know in my heart that they are no better than I am and wonder why their children deserve a better chance at growing up in life receiving a mother's love when mine couldn't.

"And most of their baby's momma's are sluts," I told myself. "They can't even hold a candle to Dianne. Still, they live and she had to die."

Inside my mine I feel a plan formulating. I don't have an answer for everything but I do know that someone has to pay.

"Who better than the chicken heads that walk around here thinking that they're the shit when in reality they really ain't shit?" I ask myself.

I know that I'll find no answers.

Check the ballistics, like Flavor Flav used to say.

Most of these bitches don't work at all or some minimum wage job. They get food stamps, free childcare, free housing, child support, and many of them at the end of the damned year get a tax refund.

What the fuck?

How many niggas buss their ass for hours upon hours,

days upon days, month upon months, year after year only to take home a couple hundred dollar tax refund?

These damned bitches barely work twenty hour work weeks and they're bringing home thousands of dollars.

And for what?

Yeah. They're primed to be my victims.

Those bitches don't have shit on Dianne and they're still here polluting this earth and giving us their asses to kiss.

It's my duty to do a public service to get rid of their asses.

I may not have all the particulars together in my head but I know I'll come up with something.

I'll have all the power. I'll be king for more than just a day.

And what about them?

Fuck them.

They don't deserve the loose, tainted spittle hanging on my tongue.

They don't deserve to enjoy the life that was taken away from Dianne.

You know what? And they won't. Believe that!

'Cause now I have the power. Peep game, real niggas do real things and I need my dick to do it. That will be an integral part of my scheme.

Less than a day and I'm out of here. I can't fucking wait.

CHAPTER ONE

Rumors

As I pounded away on the nameless face and uninspiring body laying underneath of me I knew that Miss Whatchamacallit's sexual prowess wasn't even in the vicinity of what Diane used to do for me. Miss Whatchamacallit, Miss Victim Number Six since I'd been released from prison after maxing out on my parole violation looking for answers, justice, and anything else that could explain why Diane and Michael Junior had to both die in childbirth was as good a victim as any.

Granted, it was I that gave Diane HIV which led to complications with her pregnancy and ultimately her death as well as Michael Junior's. But I can't see how the planetary rulers and those that dish out the justice were able to punish my son and his mother/my lover for my indiscretions. Why did they have to die due to my choice to lead a down low lifestyle?

As far as I'm concerned, the planetary rulers punished two innocent victims that were very dear to me so I had the power to punish those that the planetary rulers and their loved ones would consider to be innocent victims. An eye for an eye and a tooth for a fucking tooth.

I decided to be the arbiter of all justice. No one cared about what happened to my child and former lover so why should I care about anyone else?

Miss Whatchamacallit's squirming and grinding underneath of me proved that oftentimes a man's body parts circumvent his mind. In other words, my brain was rushing to my dick. The head that didn't reside on my shoulders was about to release its fluids inside of Miss Victim Number Six. Her destiny was about to be the same destiny as my unborn child's. Yes, it will take a while for this unnamed bitch to be taken out of the game. But, it is what it is. She will suffer the same fate. Science says so and I say so. Far as I'm concerned that's all that fucking matters.

***

My big dick bounces against my thigh as I walk around my apartment naked, thrilled that Miss Whatchamacallit got out of my place and off of my damned nerves. I'm anxious to wash her scent from my body so I carefully adjust the temperature of my shower water. Satisfied that it will be as hot and spicy as my skin can stand, I saunter over to my radio to get my daily fix of Miss Jones, the morning jock on Hot 97 in the New York Metro area.

To my surprise, the caller on Miss Jones's show has a voice that sounds very familiar to me. More importantly, the reason for her call stops me in my tracks.

"I swear, Miss Jones, he had unprotected sex with me knowing he got HIV It was almost like he infected me on purpose."

"Well, what's his name?" Miss Jones asks. "I wanna protect my listeners from his nasty behind."

"His name is Michael, I think," said the caller. "But I'm pretty sure he gave me the wrong last name. I haven't been able to find any information on him."

"Well, where'd you meet him?" Miss Jones asks.

"I met him at a club," the caller says. "And I saw him damned near every day until I gave his ass some. After we took off the condom in our relationship he changed his phone number and everything. I went to his place but he doesn't answer the door. Now I ain't even sure he lives there. I went there a couple times but honestly we spent more time at my place when we were seeing each other. So, I'm sure he did this outta spite. Why else would he do this to me as much as I was there for him? He must have a thing against women."

"Well, we can't give out his address or personal information over the air for legal reasons," Miss Jones says, "but trust, I promise you that I will get to the bottom of all of this."

All of a sudden I felt numb. I knew for a fact now that Miss Victim Number Two owned the voice I was hearing over the radio.

We met at an industry party in Elizabeth, N.J. about eight months ago. I was doing security and she was in there looking drunker than a motherfucker but sexy nonetheless.

I would have never stepped to her 'cept for the fact that the resemblance between her and Diane was striking. Her eyes were mesmerizing. Her figure- striking. Her face was to die for. And although I didn't figure it out until months later, her pussy was as good as I remembered Diane's to be.

For a long time I wondered if the masters of the universe were playing tricks with me. Did they dig Diane up from outta her grave and force me to deal with her again? To look in her eyes again? To deceive her again and make her suffer again? Was Miss Victim Number Two presented to me to haunt me? Was she the tool that God, if there even was a God, used to get me to detour off of my path of damage at the infancy stages of my wrath, before I inflicted too much pain on my would be innocent victims and their families?

What I know is, Miss Victim Number Two almost torpedoed my plans. She had too much class. How come she couldn't just give up the pussy easy like the rest of these sluts out here? Why'd she have to make me work for it?

Truth be told, I started digging her. Days started feeling not even worthwhile if I didn't get a chance to see her sparkling smile light up my universe. And when I wasn't with her, I felt a need to talk to her on the phone 'til the wee hours of the morning.

Like Diane, Miss Victim Number Two had never given another man oral sex before meeting me. Matter fact, she'd only had two sexual partners prior to me. She was a very virtuous woman that had the physical adornments to make any normal man happy as hell.

Aside from her body and stunningly beautiful face, Miss Victim Number Two was one of the two most supportive women I've ever met in my life. Of course, the other woman was Diane.

Miss Victim Number Two was a true friend and confidante that I treasured in every way. Why the fuck did she make me fall in love with her? Once I did, I knew that was the beginning of the end.

Yes I loved Miss Victim Number Two but I had to be honest with myself. I could never love her as much as I loved Diane and Michael Jr. Being the ghost of Diane just didn't measure up to being Diane in the flesh.

Not to mention, being saddled with guilt is one of the biggest factors that a man has in his life that makes him want or feel the need to do some wrong shit. Mainly, guilt is a sexual stimulant.

I know, I know, Miss Victim Number Two had some good ass pussy. I already said that. But, the demonic thoughts in my head kept telling me that as a Black man in America that put up with all types of bullshit on a day to day basis I deserved to get my dick sucked any time that I saw fit. It was bad enough that I was accepting that she wasn't a master at it. How the fuck was she ever gonna get better at it if she didn't practice more often?

Yeah, women will say that I was fucked up for going astray after all the big shit that Miss Victim Number Two did for me. But, they have to admit that it was her fault I went out there in search of some brain. Trust me, ladies, if you don't suck your man's dick the next woman will. Or if you're in the same boat as Miss Victim Number Two was, the next man will.

My saying that everything was Miss Victim Number Two's fault goes deeper than you may imagine. I never understood her argument that she didn't like the taste a condom left in her mouth, not even the flavored ones.

"And I ain't sucking your dick without a condom just like I ain't fucking you without a condom," she used to say. "We ain't committed to each other like that and I don't recall us ever discussing being exclusive with each other."

So, in my defense, she pushed me get somebody else to slob my knob. Granted, I was falling for her and I was falling for her hard. But, I didn't want to lose sight of the reason I was fucking her in the first place: she had to pay for the fate that the rulers of the universe dished out to Diane and Michael Jr., she had to pay just like everyone else had to pay. And it was just a matter of time before I was going to be able to feel her already bomb-ass feeling pussy totally raw. Her words and actions told me so. All I had to do was be calm and wait it out.

In the process of waiting it out, Miss Victim Number Two used some of her connections with her state job to get my juvenile records expunged not sealed and she made my adult criminal records disappear.

I can't imagine how she did it. I took the position of don't ask don't tell just like the military.

In the back of my mind I figured that she would get

fired if the stuffy shirts above her ever discovered what she did. But, I told myself that I couldn't get all teary eyed over the shit.

How often does a criminal ass nigga like myself that's been a criminal for his entire life get to see his felonies as well as misdemeanors disappear like someone was performing a magic trick?

I'll tell you how often, the answer is never.

If Miss Victim Number Two giving me a second chance in life wasn't enough for you, maybe you'll be moved when you find out that she also took out a loan against her State Pension to pay for me to go to barbershop and cosmetology school so that I could become licensed and certified. She said to me that no one could live off the little bit of money that I was making as a security guard. We had a lengthy conversation about my likes and dislikes and what would be my dream job. Then, when she found out how much I loved doing hair and make-up on both men and women, she asked me why I didn't just go to school so that I could do what I wanted to do in life.

Yeah, you're probably thinking like I was thinking that Miss Victim Number Two had a highly simplistic view of life. I'm realistic enough to know that just because you want something doesn't mean that you're going to get it. We argued for an entire week about that topic until she finally proved me wrong by cooking me a candlelight dinner one night and placing a check for thousands of dollars in my hand.

"Nobody should be doing something that they don't want to do just because," she said. "You're a very smart person and you're also giving. Why should you have to suffer your entire life just because you had a rough start? Baby, I love you and I want you to know that I don't just talk a good game. I put my money where my mouth is. If you don't get anything else out of this relationship at a minimum I hope that you figure out that everyone in the world is not 'fucked up' as you say. Some people are truly in your corner and some people really do care about you. Because I care about you, I'm giving you a chance to start all over. Put all of those fucked up demons behind you and move on with your life. Good luck, Baby, with your schooling. I'm sure you're gonna do well."

As if that was enough for you to think that I should feel like shit, something else happened that night. Miss Victim Number Two sucked my dick for the first time without a condom. She sucked my dick and when I came in her mouth she swallowed every drop.

Then she never allowed me to get totally soft. She sucked and sucked until I was once again hard as a rock. She eased my dick out of her mouth, smiled as it stood straight in the air, then climbed on it and rode me as if she were getting inspiration from an R Kelly song trying to go half on a baby with me.

Come to think of it, I did come inside of her pussy that night. Though I've never admitted it to now, that night she surpassed the best sex I'd ever had with Diane. I knew that there was only one thing left for me to do.

You guessed it: I left her ass. But I didn't leave her without emptying her purse of the additional $5,000 she had borrowed from her State Pension to take the trip to South Africa she'd always dreamed of taking.

She was to go to the travel agent the next day to make the reservations for both of us.

"I swear, Baby," she had said. "This trip is just what we need to help clear your mind and get you focused before you take this new step in your life. You and I both will get to step foot in the cell that Nelson Mandela laid his head in for years before he was released."

True, her intentions were good. Matter fact, they may have been impeccable. But, Miss Victim Number Two should have just understood that I'm a nigga from the streets and my life is gonna be whatever it's gonna be.

Besides, it took me a long time- a very long time, but in the end I did what I set out to do. I allowed my bodily fluids to be transferred from me to her.

My tryst with Miss Victim Number Two was over and it was time to move on to my next victim whether I was in love or not.

Like I said, it was all her fault. If she would' a gave me the pussy easily like she was supposed to neither one of us would have ever caught any feelings, she would still have her money, and giving her HIV would have been the only thing that I did wrong to her.

But, you can't tell a bitch nothing. They talk and talk and talk, always digging a bigger ditch for themselves. They always want to be right and can never accept when they're wrong.

Miss Victim Number Two told me before that God had big plans for me and that I would move a lot of people to make positive changes in their lives.

I remember saying, "Bitch, please. I'm just a nigga from the projects. That's how I was born and that's how I'm gonna die."

Judging from some of the on air comments of Miss Jones and her listeners, I can easily predict that I may die a lot sooner than I thought I was going to.

Miss Victim Number Two took me on a walk down memory lane today. She probably also caused some people that I couldn't escape from as easily as I escaped from her to start putting two and two together and walking, skipping, or jumping down the yellow brick road that led to either my death or dismemberment.

My days here are definitely numbered. I need to come up with a game plan as quickly as possible. Otherwise, my ass is grass.

Don't count me out, though. As I said, I'm a nigga from the street. We survive natural disasters like roaches. Of course I'm gonna survive my secret possibly being compromised.

Don't believe me then watch my work.

***

"Flim Flam!" I yelled to Freddie as he answered the phone.

"Don't start with me, Miss Thing," Freddie said in response to my chicanery. Not even ten seconds on the phone and I was already working his nerves.

Freddie Fleming is the one person that stopped me from living as a totally straight man after getting out of prison for my parole violation. I met him shortly before I started doing my bid and damn if I didn't run back into to him when I got locked up. It was there that I gave him the nickname he hates: Freddie Flim Flam.

I call him Freddie Flim Flam because back then he was always involved in one scheme or another. He'd be scheming people out of their dirty drawers right now if it wasn't for the fact that his baby's mama got all fucked up on that crack pipe. I guess knowing that his daughter needed him to step up and be a good father to her toned down his criminal ways.

"I can't be getting locked up for this petty shit," I remember Freddie saying when he learned that his baby's mama was selling off her food stamps as soon as she got them and disappearing, leaving his daughter with some of everybody.

That's part of the reason I left Freddie alone. Neither one of us look like the type of dude you'd think is gay if you saw us on the street. I didn't want people to start throwing slurs if they saw us spending too much time together. Besides, he was only my oral fix when Miss Victim Number Two wasn't getting it done for me far as sucking my dick is concerned. Yeah, I was feeling him, but he was never meant to be in the driver's seat with me. He was just a sidepiece that I'd saved the complications of getting drawn in too deep with me for his daughter's sake. But now I needed him so I had to stop caring about that bratty ass little bitch. To thine own self be true is what I think they call it.

"So, what makes you call me, Miss Thing?" Freddie

asks.

"What? I can't call you?" I respond.

"Come on now," Freddie says. "How long has it fucking been?"

"What's the problem?" I ask. "You missing having my dick in your mouth?"

"Mmm," Freddie says. "You always were a dick tease. My mouth ain't the problem. That's your thing. But I think this tight ass could use some work."

"How's Sarah?" I ask.

"What made you ask about her?" Freddie says. "You can't stand my piece of shit baby's mama. Come to think of it, I can't stand her ass either."

"I'm trying to find out if she's gotten herself together yet," I say. "I want us to go to Baltimore to handle some business."

"What? Are you running away from something?" Freddie asks. "We haven't been on the phone five minutes and someone has been blowing up your other line. How many times has it clicked?"

"Look at you all Inspector Gadget and shit," I say.

But I knew he was right. They were digging into my shit on the radio. I got a couple calls before I reached out to Freddie. Just people being nosy and shit.

"Yo, that sounds so much like you," this one or that

one hollered out over the phone to me while laughing hysterically. "Good thing your ass ain't gay but I don't know." I stopped answering. But that didn't stop people from calling me. I wasn't sure if I was in the process of being outed. But what I was sure of is that I wasn't planning on sticking around to find out.

Besides, I ain't fucking gay. Sure, I dibble and dabble a little bit but that's my damned business.

People are too damned nosy nowadays. I'm so fucking glad that Freddie doesn't listen to Miss Jones. We used to argue about him waking up to Talent on 105. Now I'm glad that he does or he may be on the same type of shit that everybody else is on calling my ass clowning me this morning.

Far as I'm concerned, what he doesn't know can't hurt him. Or in this case, it can't hurt me.

Again, I'm the only important number in this equation. I'm prominent, dominant, and everything else. Fuck Freddie, fuck Sarah, and fuck their little daughter. As long as I'm ok that's all that matters.

"So, what's up, Freddie?" I ask. "Are you game?"

"You know I am but I have to work some things out," Freddie says. "You know Sarah be fucking up and I have my daughter to worry about."

"You're right," I say. "That's why I asked about Sarah,

genius. I was hoping she got herself together." I lie. Really, I could care fucking less. "Well, you handle that and get back to me. Baltimore is gonna always be there. You only have one daughter."

I fed Freddie some more bullshit before hanging up with him. I acted like I cared about his situation when I really didn't give a fuck. It was just politically correct to put it out there like that.

In the end, I knew Freddie was gonna jump burning hoops to go to Baltimore with me. I was just having fun but he's fucking sprung.

Truthfully, what he is is just a necessary component in my plan to open a salon in Baltimore. He has the legal ride. I don't. He has the cash. I don't. And in case he gets shit fucked up and doesn't let me be the boss of things he knows that I am, he has the criminal records and warrants. I don't.

Looks like for me all the Asteroids are lining up in my favor.

***

"Hello. May I speak to Mr. Strickland?" I ask.

"May I tell him who's calling?" Tina Vasquez asks.

Tina Vasquez, nicknamed Tina Big Ass by me, is the receptionist at the Parole Office.

I know that she knew it was me as soon as she heard my voice since I knocked her off a couple times. But, she asked just to sound professional and not pressed even though she knows damned well that she is pressed. She wants some more of this dick so bad the words are probably on the tip of her tongue and dying to come out despite her being at work.

That's why I had Mr. Strickland talk to her before. She was almost on her stalker type shit so I had to tone that shit down. A player like me can't have nobody playing me so close.

"Get your shit off and get to getting," is what I always say. Why stay around with all that bonding and touchy feely shit?

"So, what made you call today, Mr. Fraser?" Tina asks. "I thought you were off parole."

"Look at this bitch being nosy," I think to myself before saying to her, "Actually, I was calling to help y'all out. I may have some information that he's interested in knowing."

"Ok, hold on," Tina says. "I'll transfer you. But, you don't have to be a stranger."

"I won't be," I say, lying.

"Good," she says before I hear a double click and the

dumb ass elevator music that used to irk the shit out of me before.

"Hello, Mr. Fraser," Strickland says. "What's on your mind? I hope you're not involved in any illegal activities."

"No. Not me," I say, sounding phony. "I'm about to go to cosmetology school and move out of state. I'm getting my life together. I don't even want to be around some of the old crew that's doing the same old things. I'm back on the right track and want to stay on the right track."

"That's good to hear, so good to hear," Strickland says.

"I've been doing this for years and not many people learn from their mistakes. You're one of my biggest success stories."

"Well, you taught me a lot," I say. I know I have to stroke his ego to get what I want. "And I'm a better person because of it. That's actually why I called you. I was hoping that one of my old buddies would get himself together. I wanted to check on him before I left."

"Is he one of my parolee's?" Strickland asks.

"Yeah," I say. "His name is Freddie Fleming.

"Freddie Fleming, funny you would call about him," Strickland says. "I'm this close to violating his ass."

"Don't tell me he's messing up," I say, trying to sound concerned.

"Rumor has it that he's associating with crack addicts,"

Strickland says.

Undoubtedly he's talking about Sarah. Strickland wouldn't know his head from his ass if someone labeled them both with black Magic Markers. But, I head to continue to plant the seeds of doubt about Freddie in his head that I called to plant.

"Wow, then it's true," I say. "I heard that too. I hope he doesn't get back on that shit, sorry stuff. He's been clean for too long."

"Well, he's good for now because so far his urine has been clean," Strickland says. "But I'm watching him with my third eye."

There goes Strickland's corny ass trying to sound hip again.

"I guess I'll do some investigative work on my own, then," I say. "If I find anything out I'll let you know. But, I can't promise you that it will be right away. It takes time to get people to talk to you about other people's business on the streets."

"Don't I know it," Strickland says. "But, its not like I ain't swamped with tons of other cases. I'll just sit his folder in the pile I have for convicts that would be violated if it weren't for the fact that I'm trying to help people not hurt them."

"The shame of it all is he really believes that," I think.

"If you find out anything just call me," Strickland says, continuing.

"I'll definitely do that," I say. "I want to see Freddie get his life together." I'm really laying the shit down thick.

"I'm proud of you, Fraser," Strickland says. "Keep up the good work."

"I have no choice," I say. "You have to grow up sooner or later.

I hang up the phone with Strickland knowing that if Freddie fucks up a warrant for his arrest is just a phone call away.

My relocation plans are fully in motion. No, you can't run away from your problems. But, no one in Baltimore will know a thing about the rumors that have undoubtedly started floating around about me since Miss Victim Number Two aired our dirty laundry on the morning show.

A player has to be a player. It's in my blood. Guess it's time for me to get some hoes in a different area code. A Baltimore bitch is still a bitch so she has to pay like the rest of them.

One thing for certain and two things for sure, my New York City secret will be safe and sound in Baltimore.

CHAPTER TWO

HBS (Homo Beauty Salon)

"So, what should we call it?" Freddie asked.

"HBS," I said.

"HBS?" Freddie said while looking confused. "What kind of damned name is that for a beauty salon?"

"A truthful one," I said. "It stands for Homo Beauty Salon." Freddie looked at me like I was crazy. "For real, it is what it is. If it looks like a duck and quacks like a duck, call it a duck."

"You have lost your damned mind," Freddie said.

"Whatever," I responded.

There was no use in even arguing about it. I knew I was gonna get my way. I was so confident that I called the sign company and placed the order with Freddie standing right in front of me.

"It feels good to be the boss of him," I thought to myself.

Freddie and I drove out to Baltimore about two months before we opened HBS in his Q5 Infiniti. Truthfully, besides his daughter I think that car is the only thing that Freddie loves more than I am.

He has thousand dollar rims on each twenty-two inch tire. There is a DVD player in the headrest of both seats. He even has infrared lights coming out of the bottom of the car that he turns on every night.

The car is definitely his showpiece. It may be the only piece of property that Freddie is defiant enough about to put in his name. Everything else he owns is in his mama's name, save for this salon. Despite his twenty thousand dollar investment compared to my two thousand, this baby is all mine. That's what the paperwork says and that's what I say. It's just a matter of time.

I talk really grimy about Freddie but the truth be told, we have grown a lot closer since the day I called him up after hearing people say bad shit about me on the radio. We were together back then almost everyday in Harlem before coming out here, now we live together.

Yes, we call ourselves roommates but that's only for show. We're not one hundred percent certain that we want to come out of the closet yet. Actually, I'm the one that's not certain. Freddie is dying to let the world know that I'm all his.

However, while Freddie is going out of his way to convince me that world should know I'm his, I'm going out of my way to convince the world that I'm anybody and everybody's.

I'm almost to the point where I'm losing count of the number of female victims that have felt my wrath.

There was the female realtor named Jackie. She had a short Toni Braxton cut with a cute face and amazing dimples. Her ass was fat like I like and her tits were somewhere in the area of Anna Nicole Smith's, rest her soul. The kicker, though, was her small waist. How a woman can have an ass like that and still fit inside a pair of size three jeans I'll never know.

Anyway, she was flirting as she showed us the space for HBS. I don't think she meant any harm. Since she's cute she was probably just using her womanly assets to get the commission.

But Jackie had no idea who she was fucking with. I'm a player among all players and I needed her to know that she had to respect that.

Plus, she was young and intelligent with her entire life ahead of her, kind of like how Dianne was before I infected her? Why should Jackie live out all of her American dreams when Dianne was taken away from me for no reason?

I was determined that Jackie's dreams would be cut short just like Dianne's were. And, since she was cute and sexy, I decided to have a little fun in the process.

I remember plopping her ass up on my new canopy bed that I'd acquired compliments of Freddie. I had her face down and ass up and was admiring how pure her tiny pussy looked from behind.

Her slim waist being in direct contrast to her apple bottom, jiggly-ass made me think I was looking at an upside down heart.

We fucked for hours while Freddie was in the other room having a temper tantrum. I could hear him blasting his music just to be smart. Then he'd turn it all the way off and pace up and down the hallway, walk up and down the stairs, basically do anything to signal to me that he knew what I was doing in my room.

Jackie thought it was cute. She assumed that Freddie was jealous and only wanted to be included in our sexual tryst. She couldn't have been more wrong.

During the dreadful, pillow talk time that followed my nutting on Jackie's face, I learned that she had only had sex one other time in her life- the night of her prom.

That explained why she was so hesitant about some of the freaky suggestions that I made while we were doing the do. It also clued me in on why she tried to scratch my eyes out when I came on her face.

"Go get me a fucking towel, NOW!" she had hollered.

It's funny thinking of it now but at that time Jackie was definitely not in the mood for fun and games.

She was a sheltered preteen and teenager. She was the product of a broken home and raised by a successful mother who's a junior partner in a prestigious Baltimore law firm.

Jackie absolutely adored her dad. She relished the weekends she spent with him in Virginia. That's actually the reason she went to Norfolk State. She wanted to be closer to him.

He bought her a car for her sweet sixteen party and lied about giving her gobs of money any chance that he got.

Jackie's mother thought she was too spoiled so her father should fall back on the uppity lifestyle that he was affording her. But he wasn't having any parts of that. Far as he was concerned, Jackie was his only child and he was going to give her any and everything that she wanted.

I guess her lack of struggle and the resulting lack of street smarts meant that Jackie couldn't protect herself from a nigga like me. But, she wasn't the first and she won't be the last.

Jackie did teach me something that was very important:

Freddie wasn't mentally stable enough to deal with me sleeping with other people. I couldn't fuck any other chicks at our place. I had to do my dirt in seamy hotel rooms like everybody else.

Oh my God he was such a bitch after that shit happened with Jackie. He walked around for days and days pouting. I had to actually end up sucking his dick to take the edge off. That was supposed to be my treat not his. But, I'm glad I did let him cum in my mouth for once. The way he treated me so special after making him feel good in that way showed me that I had even more power over him than I thought I had. I just rolled up my sleeves and filed that thought away in my mental banks so that I could put it to good use when I needed to.

***

When I needed to use the information came shortly after we opened the salon. Freddie must have gone to gay rights rallies or something because our clientele turned out to be at least seventy percent gay.

I wondered if he let people in on the secret meaning behind the name of our business, which was supposed to nothing more than a joke. Well, Freddie was taking it very seriously.

How was I supposed to continue dishing out my wrath to bitches if most of the bitches that came into HBS were carpet munchers?

Something had to give. But I didn't have time to wait for it to happen naturally. As I'd been doing my entire life, I knew I had to make shit happen.

"Whack!"

"Michael what the fuck is wrong with you?" Freddie asked after I slapped the shit out of him.

"I know what you're fucking doing, Flim Flam," I say. "I'm not as dumb as you may think."

"Miss Thing you have lost your mind," Freddie says. "I have no idea what you're talking about."

"You're trying to cut me out, don't act stupid," I say. "That's the reason you have all these gay flames walking around here. You want to pick and choose your new lover because you call yourself getting rid of me."

"Oh my God, is that what this is about?" Freddie says. "Boo, you know I love you."

"Don't fucking Boo me," I holler. "Like I said, I already told you I ain't stupid."

"Michael, you're the one all up in all these weave wearing bitches faces," Freddie says defiantly. "I'm not the one with a wandering eye and overused dick."

"Oh, so that's it," I say. "You call yourself getting back

at me. You're trying to force me out of the closet. I told you that I'd come out in due time. But, for now I have my reasons why I can't."

"Well, your reasons are your reasons," Freddie says. "Don't get mad at me if they give you a guilty conscience."

"Bottom line is whatever you're doing to have all of these gay motherfuckers in here, fall back," I yelled.

"Michael, when you say gay motherfucker, I hope you know that you're talking about me," Freddie says with sadness in his eyes. "Being gay may be part of your lifestyle but it's all of mine. If you don't accept that then you don't accept me."

Michael walks away sadly. At this point I know that he's too far gone. I can't use sex or cute pet names or anything to control him enough to come down off the ledge. All there's left to do is to do what I gotta do.

"We'll finish this later, Freddie," I say, brushing past him lovingly as I walk by. "I have to go out and take care of some business."

I walk around the corner to a secluded spot. A small part of me feels like shit but more of me knows that it's time. There's no reason to shuck and jive and act like this wasn't what it was all along.

I whip out my cell and scroll through my electronic phone book, pressing send when I find the number that

I'm looking for.

"Hello, may I please speak to Mr. Strickland," I say when Tina answers the phone. "It's Michael Fraser."

"Hello, Michael, how are you?" Tina says. "I hear you're doing big things out of state. Hold on one second and I'll get him. But don't hang up when you're done. I'd like to talk to you for a few minutes when you're done with Mr. Strickland."

"Sure, why not?" I say although my mind is saying, "Yeah! Right!"

Why the fuck would I talk to her nosy ass and clue people in on where I am and what I'm doing?

I'll pass.

All I need to do is finish cultivating the seeds that I planted months ago when Strickland gets on the phone.

In less than a week, I'll be pimping the Q5 Infiniti. Freddie is a fugitive from justice and the state of Maryland doesn't take kindly to those types of people running amuck within its borders.

Besides, Freddie said he was calling back to New York in a couple weeks to have his daughter sent out here.

He knows too many fucking people for that to happen. Next thing you know they'll be putting two and two together and figuring out that I'm out here with him.

Nah, I'll pass.

His ass needs to go on ice for a little while. I feel bad for his daughter but she's a brat anyway. She can't stand me and I don't care much for her either.

He should have been making contingency plans for her anyway. He has me to deal with.

Why should my life be altered and threatened over his dumb-ass daughter?

My daughter is dead. I don't weigh him down with my grief so why should I be weighed down by his?

"Mr. Fraser," Strickland says interrupting my thoughts. "Hi, Mr. Strickland," I say. "We have to talk. I know it's been some time but I called just like I said I would."

CHAPTER THREE

It's Our Anniversary

It has been a year since Freddie and I opened the doors of HBS. Now Freddie is just a distant memory to me.

I do appreciate him, though. When his whole arrest thing and expedition hearing went down, I acted as supportive as I could. I didn't even have to coax him into signing the title of his Infiniti over to me so that he wouldn't lose it. It was his idea.

In some strange sort of way, I'll always have a perverted sort of love for him. He helped get me on my feet. Now I'm living life the way that it should be lived: impeccably. I have a caterer coming to the shop to drop off some finger foods for my anniversary celebration. Jerk chicken wings, butterfly shrimp, Cajun style catfish nuggets with hush puppies, and fried macaroni and cheese- similar to what's sold at Friday's- are just a few of the things that are on my menu.

I also have a bar set up in the room I had added on to the shop a couple months ago. Dimples, a gorgeous little hottie that reminds me of Melissa Ford has been raking in the dough for me since I came up with the idea to have the women get their buzz on while they're waiting rather than becoming the whiny, nerve wracking little bitches they can be when they're in the salon for too long.

Today, though, Dimples will be serving up free drinks in lieu of the celebration. I'll have to put a time limit on it for sure. You know how greedy-ass niggas can get when they see some free shit.

I have eight full time stylists, not including myself, and four part timers that only work on the money days, Thursday, Friday, and Saturday. The full time stylists pay me forty dollars a week for rent plus twenty-five percent of the fees charged to their customers. Part timers pay me thirty-five percent but they don't have to pay any rent. Both full and part timers get to keep all of their tips.

In one of the rooms upstairs, we have five barbers. They pay fifty dollars a week for rent and ten percent of their gross from haircuts. Most of the time their clients are harassing Dimples in the bar area so I installed an intercom system for them. The barbers have to put money in a pot, one-hundred-dollars a week until the money I put out for it is paid back.

I have two Dominican stylists, Katrina and Evelyn that do this treatment called a Doobie. Let me tell you, they clean up.

A Doobie is a basically a wrap that's set under extreme, ungodly heat in a hair dryer that gets hot enough to fry chicken to a crisp. To say that tiny beads of sweat forming on every woman's head that sit under those hair dryers is more than an understatement.

But, after the painstaking procedure is done, the Black women's hair become straighter than I've ever seen, without a knot or nap to be found anywhere up in their kitchen. For the thirty bucks, they charge for Doobies, their clients think they're getting a steal.

For the most part Katrina and Evelyn are the most peaceful women you'd ever want to meet. Nevertheless, I can't tell you how irked they get when the hair washing girls show up late or decide to call out without telling anyone at all.

When you have ten or more women waiting to get their hair done, having good hair washers to prep your clients is invaluable. Deja is ok but only because she has to be. Her mom, Lisa, is one of the stylists here so Deja is always on point when it comes to her hours. If you've ever heard Lisa bitch and moan you'd be on point too. I'm sure that Deja wouldn't want to hear her mom's mouth if Katrina and

Evelyn started complaining to me about her hair washing, which would make me complain to Lisa then Lisa get in her shit. Everybody knows that shit rolls downhill.

I've added another hair washer named Melisa. Actually, she's a part time stylist that is filling in as the hair washer as well until she builds her clientele.

Things have been working out well over the last two weeks. I don't hear a peep out of Katrina and Evelyn on the busy days so that says something. At a minimum, Melisa is always on time or early, so they can't bitch about that.

Still, I have my eye on Melisa. She could be just acting the way that she's acting to give a good impression. Then once I fall back from sweating her so hard her true colors may come out.

The other five stylists I have are Brooklyn, Princeton, ATL, Chi-town, and Journey. It doesn't take a rocket scientist to figure out that they want people to call them by the nickname of their hometowns, thinking that will lead to more business. Far as Journey, she's a military brat so we don't know where the fuck she's from. I guess she's from everywhere.

The other three part timers are Slanted Eyes, Bijuani-the girl everyone just calls Buji since she acts so stuck-up, and Bmore. Of course you have to have the local girl that brings more drama into the shop than a little bit.

The barbers are Rick, Ronny, TT, Peabo, and Philly. All day I'm constantly telling them to calm down. Those niggas are louder motherfuckers screaming up a storm at a Ku Klux Klan rally. We can hear them all the time over the music that's so loud by the way that I'm cursing them out about turning it down four or five times each and every day.

We have our moments but really we're a tight knit group of hair professionals that have formed a bond that's sort of like a family. Everybody knows that you can't have a chip on your shoulder for too long against someone that you have to see everyday. It's better if you just squash the bullshit to make sure your work environment isn't stressful. That will help you to live a lot longer, believe me.

***

The gang has piled in and I've smacked hands I don't know how many times over them trying to eat up all the damned food before the customers and more importantly local radio station gets here.

I booked the midday jock to come out and do an on location, live broadcast from HBS for two hours. Yes, I'm pulling in the maximum amount of dollars for this location but I am thinking of expanding.

I need this spot to start looking like Puerto Ricans in a station wagon to get a few of the stylists frustrated enough to venture out and open new hair terrain. For me that would mean, Mo Money, Mo Money, Mo Money!

My dream of expansion doesn't seem too farfetched judging from all the women and Wannabe ballers that are packed up inside HBS. I can't tell you how many times I've said today, "This ain't just the hangout spot; I hope that everybody that's here is getting something done to their hair."

I went as far as to have Melisa go around and hand out numbers to people, collecting a fifty percent deposit on whatever it is they're having done, just to make sure that trespassers aren't just here for the free food and drink. Trifling. Niggas are just like vultures. You already know how many motherfuckers left when she asked them to dig in their pockets. But, since it's still crowded as hell here I'd say that I can pat myself on the back for a very successful year.

"I'm now with the owner of HBS, Mr. Fraser," the local midday Jock named Zooman says, catching me off guard.

"Fraser," I cut in quickly.

"Ok, Fraser," Zooman says. "What made you name the salon HBS?"

If Zooman caught me by surprise before his question has me totally shook.

"Aahh, Ummm, I'm not really sure," I say.

"Mmm Hmm," Zooman responds. "I'm sure that there's some deep reason that will come to the surface eventually.

At that point I was so glad that I've been able to filter in a more balanced level of clientele. Yes, we still have about thirty to forty percent gay and lesbians in our client base but it's nowhere near the approaching ninety percent gay demographics we boasted when Freddie was here.

An hour after my impromptu interview with Zooman has netted even more inquisitive minds to come into the salon. Truth be told, I can't wait for the last half and hour of the live broadcast to be over so some of these people can get the fuck out of here.

It's not like all these people can get their hair done today, anyway. It's like pulling teeth to get people to work on a Sunday but most of the staff have appointments booked for at least a half a day tomorrow. And, if you know anything about me, a weekend appointment brings in twenty percent more cash than a walk in. So, though this live broadcast has been somewhat of a pain in the ass, it's gonna make the routine ten to fifteen G's that I normally pull in on a weekly basis look like forty. I can't be mad at that.

As I'm reveling in the fact that after ten minutes all of this live broadcast nonsense will be over I notice Zooman paying special attention to the curious dude that walked in about five minutes ago.

Matter fact, many of the people in the shop are whispering and rumbling about him. This makes me curious so I move closer to Zooman so I can find out what's good with this dude.

"Well, Mr. Long, your father has been a fixture in this community for years," Zooman says. "He will be surely missed. I'm sure, though, that you'll make sure his legacy lives on."

"I'll do my best," the dude says.

"Ladies and gentleman, that was Bongo Long, son of the legendary Pastor Frederick Long of the First Abyssian Baptist Church," Zooman says. "His father's viewing is... Wait a minute. When is the viewing over?"

"You can view the body up until nine pm tonight or from nine A.M. until eleven A.M. tomorrow before the funeral starts," the dude named Bongo Long says. "Everyone is welcome. My dad had love and passion for everybody."

"There you have it," Zooman says. "Pastor Frederick Long's home going party is eleven A.M. tomorrow at the

First Abyssian Baptist Church. With everything that he's done for this community, let's make sure that we send him off well."

I'm not sure if I'm angry that this Bongo Long dude stepped on the shine HBS was getting today for my anniversary or too curious about what he and his dad mean to Baltimore to care. While I'm sorting it out, Zooman brings him my way so that he can introduce us.

"Bongo Long, I'd like for you to meet Mr. Fraser," Zooman says.

"Fraser," I say, correcting Zooman as I extend my hand.

"Bongo," says the handsome dude as he takes my hand and holds it too long to be cordial and too loosely to be acting macho. "You have a very nice establishment here. It's amazing that you've only been in business for a year."

"Thank you very much, Sir," I say. "We do our best."

"Your best looks fine to me," Bongo says. "You're gonna need oxygen masks for the people in here if it gets any more crowded."

"Yeah, thanks to Mr. Zooman my dream of expanding this salon into other locations may just be met," I say.

"Interesting," Bongo says. "You want to expand."

"You can't just rest on your laurels," I say. "We should always be looking for opportunities to do bigger and better things."

"I'll keep you in mind," Bongo says as he turns to leave then pauses. "I know you're busy today but I hope that you can stop by tomorrow for my dad's funeral."

"I have tons of appointments tomorrow as a spillover from today but I'll do everything in my power to make it," I say.

"I hope you can," Bongo replies.

I watch him walk away, curious about his handshake and curious about what he meant by he'll keep me in mind.

I don't have to wonder long, though. Zooman fills me in immediately about his take on what just happened.

"Wow, that was major," Zooman says.

"What was major?"

"I'm sure Bongo liked what he saw here and he's interested in getting a piece of the pie," Zooman replies.

I lift my eyebrows since I still don't know where Zooman is coming from.

"Come on man," Zooman says. "I'm positive he wants to invest in your expansion. You can't tell me my time here wasn't worth the money you spent. Bongo's gonna take you places you couldn't imagine."

"Is that right?" I say cause I don't know what else to say.

***

The remainder of my Saturday is hectic. Sunday follows the same suit. Still, I find time to dip in and out Pastor Frederick Long's funeral. Staying just love enough to make sure that his son Bongo notices me in the crowd.

When his eyes meet mind, I give him a nod to make sure he's seen my show of support for him. Shortly afterwards, I break out when he gets caught up in all of the details of his father's funeral that he has to attend to.

A half an hour out of my busy day wasn't so bad. Who knows what will come out of it.

For now, though, I need to get my ass back to HBS so I can tend to my clients that I left with Melisa.

Not because I think she'll do a bad job and piss someone off. I'm more worried that she'll have happy customers and drain off some of my clients from me.

You guessed it. It's all about the money with me.

You're my motherfucker, Melisa, but don't mess with my money. Keep that in mind and we can be all good in the hood.

CHAPTER FOUR

The Dark Side of HBS

Everything wasn't all good in the hood when I returned from the funeral. The radio was blaring at a deafening level and from the hollering I heard coming from upstairs I could tell that TT was letting the local riff raff gamble again on the premises.

I was sort of in a conundrum. Although the stylists do a good job, a damn good job, I wasn't too foolish not to know that half of the reason that the flyest chicks be breaking their necks to get an appointment at HBS is they know some of Baltimore's biggest ballers hang out in the barbershop room upstairs.

Truth be told, the barbers and their clients are more of a pain in the ass than anything. But, their clients keep Dimples from complaining about the scraps I pay her since they hit her off with crazy tips on the daily. And, although I turn a blind eye to the gambling and oftentimes break up games when they get out of control, I accept a minimum of $500 bucks a day in cut money, the commission that the house gets from anyone that wins a hand while playing cards or hits a number when shooting dice.

So, I battle all the time with myself, sorting out the pros and cons behind letting the barbers and their clients have the free will at times that all the stylists complain about them having.

"You can't please everyone," Is what I often say.
They know that the barbers' clients bring in the chicken-head groupies and gold diggers. They don't have to act so self-righteous with me.

But, at times the stylists do have a point about the unacceptable behavior. Like they say, give a nigga an inch and he wants a mile; give his ass a rope and he wants to be a cowboy.

"TT, what the fuck is going on?" I ask after lowering the radio to a level where he can actually here me.

"Come on, Fraser, this is the jam!" Fraser says. "You know motherfuckers love Pac. 'I get around.., round and round, round we go.'"

"They can love Pac," I say. "They can love Biggie too. But, first of all they better love my shop. You're supposed to be the supervisor up here. You're as bad as anybody else."

"My bad, Fraser," TT says. "Don't start trippin' on me." Before he can say another word I cut my eyes over to the crap game and all the yelling that I heard when I came inside the salon. "And don't worry about that. I got you," TT says.

He knows I'm about to pitch a fucking bitch.

I go back downstairs still mumbling under my breath.

To my dismay, I have the same three clients waiting since before I left. They still haven't had their hair washed or blow-dried.

"Melisa, what the fuck?" I snap.

"Don't even start with me, Fraser," Melisa responds. "That's Deja. I'm over here, remember?"

"Damn, Melisa, on a Sunday?" I say. "You know I never work on Sundays."

Melisa shrugs her shoulders. She knows I always use her for prep and only like using Deja sparingly now that she's here.

But I'm certain that the other vultures that call themselves stylists capitalized on the fact that I went to the funeral. I can't complain, though. We operate on a first come first come basis.

"Well, where is Deja?" I ask angrily.

"Don't get mad at me, Boo," Melisa says. "She's upstairs braiding somebody's hair."

"Ooh," I say loudly. "Not a fucking gain," I add under my breath.

As I stomp back up the stairs I already know what I'm gonna see.

Sure enough, when I push open the door to the hair braiding room, Deja is on her knees in front of Stacks, sucking his dick.

I quickly close the door behind me and call out to Deja vehemently though in a whisper.

"Deja, what the fuck?" I say.

She jumps up away from Stacks looking ashamed like the busted little whore that she is.

"Damn, Fraser, why you hatin'?" Stacks asks.

Let me tell you about Stacks. He calls himself that because he's delusional, thinking he makes long dough.

The truth of the matter is, I make way more money at the salon than Stacks makes selling drugs.

He calls himself a baller but he's far from it. What kind of a hustler gambles away his re-up money?

If you're a big boy in the drug game your money should never dip up and down like Stacks does. It's because he's the biggest perpetrating a fraud Wannabe hustler I ever heard of.

Not to mention that he's a trick. He's tricked away more of his drug profits than he's bought bricks with to make more profits.

He's a fucking idiot. I don't even like drug dealers. But damn if I wouldn't be a better hustler than him. He works on my last fucking nerve. Every time that I see him I have a fucking Woohsah moment.

"I'm a tell you like this, Stacks," I say. "Let me have to tell you about disrespecting my fucking business one more time. There won't be another."

"You're funny," he says as he makes himself decent and walks over near where I'm standing. "You know you gotta finish hooking me up later cause I ain't buss," he says, turning back to Deja before he leaves the room.

"What the fuck am I gonna do with you?" I ask Deja. "You know if I fire your ass your mom is gonna wanna know why, right? And what the fuck am I supposed to tell her? Should I let her know that you've been sucking these fake-ass hustlers dicks up in my shop and fucking them in their cars in the parking lot?"

Deja doesn't say a word. What the fuck could she say?

"Listen, you'd better get yourself together," I say. "I'm not gonna keep crying wolf with your ass. Sooner or later it's gonna be a wrap."

"Well, I gotta go downstairs, Fraser," Deja says. "I have to wash a few heads of your clients that are waiting."

"Yeah, you do," I say. "You shoulda at least done that

before you decided to come up here and put a dick in your mouth." She looks at me with hurt eyes. When I swing I swing hard and often below the belt. "At least if your work was done I wouldn't even have come looking for you. You would have gotten away with being a whore this time."

I'm so hard on Deja because she's a follower and not a leader. She used to have her shit together until things she saw happening that she knew she had no business getting involved in influenced her.

I'm not slow. I know that Deja wasn't the first chick to be tricking in or around my shop. I can't prove it but in my heart of hearts I know that Katrina and Evelyn are a pair of broken down madams.

Their Dominican little cousins and girlfriends come in the shop all the time keeping them company, bringing them food, and running errands for them. That in itself wouldn't be so bad if they didn't disappear for twenty minutes every time certain male clients come in the shop then come back with their hair and clothes looking disheveled.

Like I said, I ain't slow.

This type of stuff started happening months ago after Freddie, well, you know. They would have never tested him the way they test me. Not that I'm a slouch or anything but my body doesn't compare to the chiseled, hard rock figure that Freddie boasted.

Honestly, though, I don't think it's about fear. I'm pretty sure that everyone that enters HBS knows that my love for money causes me to turn my head to a lot of shit that I don't necessarily agree with.

That's the reason why although we've grown under the appearance of being a professional, urban renaissance shop, sometimes HBS is as gangster or gully as any salon can get. I wonder sometimes if that's part of the appeal of my business. If nothing else, it always seems like it's a party going on up in here.

Dimples keeps the drinks flowing. Most of the time I allow her to bring in food from home that she's prepared to sell it to our clients. And all throughout the day I'm yelling upstairs for the barbers to turn the music down.

I think the ability to drink, eat, and be merry while engaging in stimulating conversation or out and out he say she say that keeps drama going is all the ingredients a person needs for a good time.

Add to that the ability for a woman's weave to be tightened up or a man's cut to be looking fresher than a motherfucker and I can see why HBS is the place to be. No wonder why we're becoming too big for our britches and feeling cramped up like Sardines.

Success has its benefits and its challenges.

CHAPTER FIVE

Bongo & Pastor Frederick Long

As Melisa is being nice to me by giving me a neck, shoulder, and lower back massage after a grueling two days, I receive a surprise but certainly welcome visitor.

It's Bongo Long. I don't know him from Adam but I see dollar signs when I look at him.

Maybe it's because of what Zooman said or because of my expansion dreams, but whatever the case I'm happy to see him.

"I'm glad that you're still here," Bongo says. "I wanted to thank you for bidding my dad farewell. Oh yeah and I brought you something." Bongo hands me a plaque. "It was hand made in South Africa, my hometown. It represents the strength of continuing to fight and never giving up just as Nelson Mandela did while imprisoned. I felt it was an appropriate gift for a one year anniversary."

"Thank you so much," I say.

I can't front. The massage that Melisa is giving me is beyond relaxing and sorely needed. But, I'm surprised that she hasn't excused herself yet. It would be awkward for me to say something so I'm just hoping she comes up with it on her own.

Melisa ordinarily isn't the type of person that wants to be caught in the middle of two other peoples' conversation. Her favorite phrase is, "My name is Bennett and I ain't in it."

There has to be something going on with her. I'll have to ask her about it later.

"Well, I don't want to keep you long," Bongo says. "I know you've had a rough couple of days. Still, I wanted to bring you my number so that we could talk."

"Talk?" I say.

"Yes, talk business," Bongo replies. "Maybe we can have lunch or something tomorrow."

"That sounds ok to me," I say hesitantly. "Mondays are normally slow days for me. Truthfully, half the time I don't even go out of my house on Mondays. Since Melisa has been here she opens and closes the shop for me if I ask her to so I don't even have to come in if I don't want to. Oh yeah, Melisa, this is Bongo Long."

"Hello," Melisa says flatly. "Sorry for your loss."

"Thank you so much," Bongo responds. "And it's a pleasure to meet you."

I take note the fact that Bongo only holds Melisa's hand for a millisecond when he shakes her hand. This is in direct contrast to how he how mine when Zooman introduced us yesterday.

"Well, I have to be going," Bongo says. "I look forward to lunch tomorrow."

"Me too," I say.

"Bye," Melisa says flatly as Bongo walks out the door. I look at Melisa suspiciously then ask, "What was that about?"

"He's a flamer," she says.

"A flamer? What's that?" I ask.

"A flaming faggot," Melisa says.

"Melisa, that's not like you," I say. "That's the first time I've ever heard you say anything negative about a person."

"You're right," Melisa says. "I'm sorry. I try to be a good person like God would want me to be but homosexuality is wrong. But, I'll spare you my soapbox today. I'm trying to relax you with this massage not have you all tense."

"Thanks. You're the best," I say, glad that I won't have to be drawn into a conversation that I certainly don't want to have with her.

***

The Baltimore Seashore Restaurant is an elegant dining establishment that sits right on the bay. It's indoor/outdoor setting allows eaters on the deck to smell the fresh saltwater while they're sipping on the fantastic mixed drinks or chomping away at the best damned crab cakes that I've personally ever had.

I've told myself over and over that I was gonna eat here prior to today. Everyone has told me how excellent the food and drinks are. But, they've also told me about how expensive it costs here, that's why my cheap ass hasn't come here before today. The only reason that I'm here now is that Bongo is treating.

Wait. Is he treating?

"Not to make things awkward, but is this your treat?" I ask. "I don't normally come to places this costly."

"Relax," Bongo says. "Don't you know who my dad was?"

"Not really," I say. Bongo looks at me like he's surprised. "I'm just being honest," I add.

"Wow, a Black male in Baltimore that doesn't know about my dad can't be a Black man from Baltimore," Bongo says.

"I don't like talking about my past," I say, defensively.

There's no way in hell I'm gonna tell this stranger anything at all about my time in New Jersey and New York City.

"There's nothing to be ashamed of," Bongo says. "No matter what you were before now you're highly successful. That means you've beaten the odds and made something out of yourself. Your journey should make you feel even more proud of your accomplishments."

"That's one way to look at it," I say.

"Nonsense," Bongo replies. "That's the only way to look at it."

"Why did you ask me here?" I ask.

"Truthfully, I want in," Bongo says. "I want in with everything."

"Everything? All there is, is HBS," I say. "That's my pride and joy. That's all I have in this world."

"I'm sure there's more to you than that," Bongo says.

"You just don't realize your worth."

"Is that right?" I say. "What makes you think that when you don't even know me? You just met me."

"I know your workers value you," Bongo says. "How many bosses are there out here in this world that would love to have a subordinate give them a massage when they're stressed?"

"Probably a lot," I say. "But, they probably don't treat their staffs as well as I treat mine. We're all like family."

"That's exactly my point," Bongo says. "You have a caring persona. You're a humanitarian. That's worth more than all the money that you make in your salon."

"You obviously don't know me very well," I say.

"That's why we're here," Bongo says. "Maybe you'll allow me to get to know you. Maybe you'll want to get to know me."

"I'm not sure where you're going with this," I say, lying. After the handshake and Melisa's observations, I'm positive that Bongo is a gay male that calls himself macking me right now.

"First of all, I think what you've done with HBS is brilliant," Bongo says. "I want a piece of that action. I want to help you open up at least two or three more locations in DC or Virginia."

"You know it costs over twenty-thousand-dollars just to open the doors of HBS," I say. "And I've spent a lot more than that expanding the place."

"Money is not an object to me, Sir," Bongo says. "You really don't know a thing about my dad do you?"

"Can't say that I do," I respond.

"Well, to make a long story short, he's left me with millions," Bongo says.

For the first time I feel like it's ok to let my guard down. Bongo should be the one on the defensive. He's the one with deep pockets.

"So, you shouldn't be sitting here at a restaurant in Baltimore, as nice as it is," I say. "You should be somewhere traveling like on the French Riviera."

"Actually, I am," Bongo says. "But, I'm traveling in my mind. Your mind can take you further away than any plane ever can."

"So, what makes you want to get involved with HBS?" I ask, changing the subject.

"Your salon seems to have the pulse of the Black community," Bongo says. "I live for that. After the way that I was brought up I capture that sort of camaraderie any way that I can."

"Not to be getting too much in your business but it seems like you had the perfect upbringing," I say.

"Is that what you think?" he asks.

"Well, yeah!" I say.

"Well you're wrong. You're dead wrong."

I don't say anything else to him but I question him with my eyes. My silent probing causes him to open up to me.

"Well, Mr. Fraser..."

"Fraser," I say, interrupting.

"Fraser, let me tell you a few things about the honorable Pastor Frederick Long," Bongo says. "For starters, he isn't my real dad. Don't look shocked. Most of the people around here no that I'm adopted. No one would say anything, though. My dad would go off on people if they acted like I was just a stepchild. With all the bad shit that he did to me I still call him Dad. He went off on me too enough about it."

"Anyway," Bongo continues. "My dad was killed in a civil war in Africa. I was a refugee brought over here by some humanitarian worker from DC. My dad fell in love with me right away. I was only six. I was his pride and joy. His wife died before ever giving him any kids. But, I've always wondered if she pretended not to be able to be have kids because she found out about the Pastor's secret."

"Secret?" I say.

"Yeah, secret," Bongo responds. "My dad started fucking me up the ass right about the time I turned ten years old." I spit out a sip of my drink due to my shock. "Don't be appalled. It is what it is. I'm not the first little boy to be abused by a religious man and I won't be the last."

"What made you share that with me, though?" I ask. "You don't even know me."

"Well, I thought we agreed to get to know each other," Bongo says. "Besides, I feel we should be open if I'm gonna be investing a hundred-thousand-dollars into making HBS a chain of urban retro salons. I don't have anything to hide. Do you?"

"Of course not," I say. You know as well as I know that's not the truth.

"Good, then we're about to be partners," Bongo says. Out of nowhere, he starts laughing. "If you don't mind me asking, though, how long have you been fucking Melisa?" I look at him surprised.

"I do mind you asking and I've never fucked Melisa," I say.

For once I'm telling the truth.

"Well, I thought I noticed a little chemistry, that's all," Bongo says.

I take inventory of what Bongo has said and start thinking about Melisa. I haven't known her that long but it's been long enough for me to notice that she is kind of cute.

She reminds me of Tweet except she's a little thicker. I don't know what it is but a nice ass has always satisfied my urges. Melisa definitely has a nice ass.

Truthfully, Dimples and her run neck and neck as far as cuteness. Dimples is light and Melisa is brown skinned but they're both sexy as all hell.

Dimples is more like a buddy to me, though. Or maybe I'd call her a little sister.

She's about her business, very professional, but she never trespasses unto territory that most people would deem off limits.

Melisa, though, will straight get in all of your business.

"I'm your friend, right? And wouldn't you want your friend to be honest to you?" she often asks when she's walking over a line you never invited her to walk over. "I mean, the most important thing is keeping it real, right?"

She does have a style and swagger about herself that any man would find attractive. Cut and dry, I am more attracted to Melisa than I am Dimples.

That doesn't explain why I've banged Dimples out twice and never even looked at Melisa that way until Bongo mentioned it.

But, if you saw how good Dimples looked when she came in for her interview you wouldn't blame me. Plus, she was flirting with me like crazy.

"I'm good at everything I do, believe that," Dimples said while licking her lips the day that I asked her if she was any good at making drinks.

"What's that supposed to mean?" I remember asking her.

"It means whatever you want it to mean," she responded.

Ten minutes later I was fucking her in the same room that I complain to Deja about sucking hustler's dicks in.

I know what you're thinking but you're wrong. I wore

a condom when I fucked her, both times. Something told me that Dimples was gonna help me bring in a lot of extra money. If you don't know anything else about me you know I don't fuck around with my money.

"Hmm, Melisa," I thought to myself. "Interesting."

CHAPTER SIX

Betrayal

It's nine months later and things have calmed down a little on Covington Street, the original location for HBS.

By now we have one satellite location in Washington, DC and one in Arlington, Va. not far from the Pentagon. Soon we will have a location operational in the Southern portion of Virginia just outside of the U.S. Naval Base in Norfolk. At that location we'll be able to capitalize on the naval population, students that go to Norfolk State University, and visitors that are always around the nearby Virginia Beach area.

I let TT handle the DC shop since that's where he's from. Maybe the violent atmosphere of DC will help him tone down some of the activity that goes on in the shop there. He's been living in Baltimore for about ten years now so there's no way he knows as many people in DC as he used to.

It seems like Ronny has taken over the illegal activities that go on in the barbershop. Thankfully, he has a little bit more control over it than TT did. Still, they have their moments where they continue to get on my nerves. But, when speaking on getting on my nerves, lately it's definitely been the stylists.

They got real catty about who was gonna branch out and take what they all perceived to be a promotion by running the other locations. From the door, I knew I had to be really professional about the shit.

Bongo and I scheduled formal interviews. I even reviewed their attendance records and financial performance.

If they were going to be on their own without being under my watchful eye, I definitely didn't plan on having someone whose math never added up right left to their own devices at a satellite location.

When it was all said in done, I chose Chi-town to work at the DC location with TT. If any bitch is gully enough to deal with the rough and tumble of DC Chi-town is. She walks around here she's Laila Ali or something, dying for a fight.

Peabo and Bijuani appeared to be the perfect match to run the Arlington, Va. location. Since they both act so fucking stuck up they'll fit right into the neighborhood in Arlington where we leased a building.

Philly begged me to let him go to the Norfolk, Va. salon when we open it up since he's heard so much about the girls that go to Norfolk State and he's even gone to Virginia Beach for their Greek fest a couple times. Journey seemed to be the natural choice for the ladies since she fits in so well with young people and military people, both segments of the Norfolk population that makes up about eighty-five percent of the demographics that we're targeting.

Bongo actually wanted me to have Melisa run that location when it opens up but I don't know what makes him think I would want to do that. She's talented and she's loyal but she's also kind of green. She needs a little bit more time under my tutelage before I'd let her go out their running some shit.

Bongo thinks that it's a matter open for discussion but I've already made up my mind, and for business reasons only.

You can't tell Bongo that, though. He's convinced that Melisa and I have something going on. If he keeps it up, he's gonna push me into her sexy-ass looking arms. And I have a hunch that I'd be welcome by her.

Over the last nine months Melisa and I have grown very close. She's my biggest friend and confidante at the shop. And, though it's true we've done more than our share of flirting with each other, I honestly have never touched her. My main reason is Bongo and Melisa are like oil and water. They clash on everything. If I didn't leave the Covington Street location out of the partnership that I set up with him I'm sure he would have tried to fire her by now.

A part of me feels like if I gave Melisa some of this dick she'd throw it up in Bongo's face just because she thinks he has a crush on me.

God only knows what she'd do if she realized that we've been fucking now for months. Yeah, you heard right. I've put my vendetta with bitches on hold for a second and I'm in a monogamous relationship with another man. And, sometimes it's actually kind of cool being an in the closet bi-sexual. I don't care what you say, I still like pussy so my ass ain't gay.

Every chance Melisa gets she starts quoting scriptures from the Bible about homosexuality.

"I'm telling you, it ain't right, Fraser," she says. "God said to kill 'em and stone them that's how disgusted he is with gays."

"Give me a fucking break," I find myself thinking.

I don't even speak on it anymore when she goes on a tangent. I figure if I ignore her I won't give her rants any fuel and she'll just shut the fuck up.

Yet, although Melisa is loud, talkative, nosy, argumentative, and judgmental. I love her to death. That sounds funny, right, after my description of her?

But, some things you just can't explain. They are what they are. Just like our friendship is what it is. We know what each other are thinking and we finish each other's sentences. Sometimes I think we're operating with one joint mind instead of two separate entities.

Bongo can't stand it when we talk for each other. He also can't stand it when Melisa gives me massages. That's why I'm sure he'd be upset if he knew she was giving me a massage in the hair braiding room right now.

I started moving my massages up here so Bongo could stop bitching when he walks in on us. I can't understand for the life of me how we're making any money at the other two locations when most of the time he's here checking up on me, well Melisa and me.

I don't know how many times I've asked him, "Ain't you worried about making your money back? How the fuck can you do that when you're always here spying on me?"

Everybody already knows that I'm about making a dollar. All that love and sex shit is secondary.

"What the fuck?" Bongo hollers when he opens the door to the hair braiding room and sees Melisa giving me a massage. "I thought I told you to stop letting her do that shit to you."

"First of all calm the fuck down and quiet down," I say. "Secondly, you can't tell me shit about what I do in here because this is not part of the partnership. How many times have I told you that? But, even if it were part of the partnership you couldn't tell me shit. I was real clear about who was in charge when you came on board. I never left any room for error about that."

"Melisa, why don't you get out of here and let us talk?" Bongo says rudely.

"Excuse me?" Melisa spits angrily.

"Chill, I got this," I say. "You can't be coming at my assistant's neck like that, Bongo, come on now." I turn to Melisa. "With that said, can you go to Starbucks and get me a Caramel Latte Light while my partner and I work some shit out."

"Of course, anything for you," Melisa says before giving me a final rub that seems much more sexual than therapeutic. I'm sure she did it just to piss Bongo off more than he already is.

"Don't tell me you ain't fucking that bitch," Bongo says before I shush him.

Although he's already doing what he considers to be a whisper I still want him to quiet down even more. I'm very serious about my secret remaining a secret. Though it's been a few months since I've gotten down, victims eight, nine, and ten are all located in Virginia, just a hulk spit away from the Maryland border.

"I can't understand why you're dogging me like this," Bongo says. "You told me you loved me."

"Can you shut the fuck up?" I say, sounding panicky. "How many times do I have to tell you that this is my place of business?"

"Go ahead, hide me away in the corner like I'm some piece of trash," Bongo says. "You're not proud of me. The only thing that you're worried about regarding me is people's perception that you're cool with me."

"You're sounding real stupid," I say. "Where does all of this pent up anger come from?"

"It comes from the fact that I know you don't mean it when you say you love me," Bongo spits. "Do you?"

I ponder his question.

I'm positive that I love the money but I wonder if I love the man.

He does suck my dick better than anyone ever did, even better than Dee-Dee did in prison. His ass is really tight and a lot of times gets really wet like a pussy. He definitely has sexual perks that I don't have a problem with.

And what can I say about the money? Everyone knows

that I love money. Every time that I turn around he's buying me gifts. This year when I have my two-year anniversary I'll be celebrating four locations not just one. My gross income including my portion of the partnership monies from the three locations will locations will be about seven-hundred-thousand as opposed to two-hundred-thousand so there's another benefit to add to Bongo's list of advantages.

"What was I asking myself again?" I think to myself.

"I said do you love me?" Bongo asks, reminding me of the quandary I find myself in.

"I'll tell you for a fact right now I don't love you," I say.

"I'm done telling you about bringing this shit into my salon. Take your ass home and we'll talk about this later."

"You can't talk to me like that," Bongo says.

"Take your fucking ass home like I said and we'll talk about it later," I say, angrily. This time I've raised my voice and I'm clenching my fists as if I'm back in prison and getting ready for battle.

"Fine, be like that," Bongo says, relenting as he walks out the door.

Although I doubt that anyone heard us I feel too embarrassed to walk back into the populated areas of the barbershop or the salon. I try to relax myself in the hair braiding room as best as I can although truthfully the tightness in my neck tells me that I'm as stressed as ever.

"I know something has to give," I say to myself. "I can't keep putting up with this bullshit."

In a knick of time, Melisa comes back with my Caramel Latte Light.

"You looked stressed; do you need me to finish?" she asks.

"You know I do," I say.

Like magic, she digs her hands into my skin and muscles that were minutes ago pleading for her.

"You know, if I didn't know any better, I'd think you gave him some of that big dick you're always talking about," Melisa says.

"Not now, Baby," I say. "I don't need stress. I need to wind down."

I tell myself that I need to make a mental note of the fact that I keep calling Melisa, Baby. More than anything,

I have to remember to never say that shit around Bongo.

"Why do you say shit like that when you know I ain't gay?" I ask Melisa. "Is it because I never gave you none of this big dick?"

"Boy, you couldn't handle this pussy," she says, jokingly. "You're already stressed out enough as it is. You can't feel how tight the muscles are in your shoulders but I can."

"What happened to you being so righteous?" I ask. "You curse more and say more freaky shit than any Christian I've ever known."

"Well, I ain't perfect, that's for damn sure," Melisa says.

"But, I do know Jesus and I know that Jesus wouldn't approve of the way that Bongo be looking at you. It's not natural for a man to look at another man with those type of eyes. He looks at you the way that I look at you."

"Whatever. You're scared of this dick, Melisa," I say. "I mess around and give you some one day but I'm scared it would fuck with my money."

"I know, I know," Melisa says. "You never mess around with your money."

"You got that right," I say, agreeing. "Business and freaky sex don't mix. So stop tempting me. I'm a weak ass man as it is."

"I know you are, Boo," Melisa says as she bends down so that her plump titties can massage the back of my neck through her shirt.

That's all that I need to get me totally relaxed. Before I know what's hit me, I'm fast asleep.

CHAPTER SEVEN

Caught Up

I wake up mad at the fact that Melisa didn't wake me up before she left. I know she did it on purpose just to add more fuel to the fire in the argument I'm gonna have with Bongo soon as I see him later.

Well, she doesn't know that I'm gonna see him later but she did it purposely nonetheless.

I get in my car and drive until I pull onto Conway Street, not far from the Baltimore Convention Center.

The Long family has held onto a prime piece of real estate in this area for years thanks to Pastor Long's ministry. By now the house his dad left to him must be worth at least two-million-dollars to Bongo.

When I disable the alarm with the code and go inside of course Bongo is on the couch sulking.

He absolutely loves the bedroom that his dad had made especially for him so the only reason he's on the couch is so that he can be one hundred percent sure of the time I came into the house.

I hang up my keys on the plaque on the wall just like I always do when I spend the night with Bongo. Although I have my own place, I spend a lot of nights with him. It alleviates the need for a lot of arguments.

Tonight he appears to be in an especially pissy mood so I choose not to open my mouth. The last thing that I need is an argument. I decide to tread lightly on the stormy waters.

"So, you don't speak to nobody when you walk in the door?" Bongo asks, sarcastically.

"Hey," I say emotionless. I refuse to be drawn in.

"Mmm, at least Patch is happy to see me when the pet sitter brings him home from the kennel at night," Bongo says as he rubs on his mangled looking mutt's neck. "You love me don't you boy? Don't you?"

The way that Bongo interacts with his dog is sickening to me.

"Did you buy anything for dinner?" I ask.

"Mmm. I thought you would a ate some of Melisa's scraps," Bongo says.

He's pushing me really, really hard.

"How about DC and Arlington- how'd they do today?" I ask.

"Wouldn't know," Bongo says. "I ain't been there."

"You ain't been there? What do you mean you haven't been there?" I ask, becoming more and more frustrated. "Today is Friday, one of our big money days. You always have to check their banks on Fridays."

"Well, I'm not as good with that business type stuff as you are," Bongo says. "I'm more good at things like loving people the right way and treating everybody decently."

"You know what? I don't have time for this shit," I say angrily. "I'm out. It seems like you ain't in the mood and I ain't in the mood either."

I have no clue what Bongo is saying to me as I take my keys from hanging off of the plaque and walk out the door. All I know is I'm not in the mood for any bullshit tonight.

"How could that idiot not check the fucking bank?" I ask myself. "Now he's fucking around with my fucking money."

I head to the Havana Club near the Inner Harbor so I can puff on a cigar and grab myself a quick bite to eat. I'm determined that I'm going to stay in the relaxed state that Melisa put me in before she left.

"Speaking of the devil," I say to myself when I walk inside the Havana Club and see Melisa blowing circles in the air while puffing on what appears to be one of the illegal Cubans she's told me about.

"What the hell are you doing here?" I ask her.

"No, the question is what are you doing here," she says.

"You know I come here all the time."

"That's right, I forgot," I say when I notice her drink.

"I'm sure that's nonalcoholic, praise the Lord." I say, teasingly.

"You know, you need to stop sweating me about my religion and find some of your own," Melisa says. "I may slip up from time to time but I'm not overbearing with you about whatever the hell you're doing with fag boy."

"You never miss an opportunity to bring up that subject, do you?" I ask.

"You don't come at my neck and I won't come at yours," Melisa says.

"Vengeance is mine, sayeth the Lord," I respond.

"Let me find out you know one scripture out of millions," Melisa says. "You're gonna mess around and make me go into shock."

"How bout we just call it a truce," I say.

"Fine with me," Melisa says extending her hand so I can shake it.

When I do shake her hand she holds onto it in the same manner that Bongo did the day I first met him.

"What do you want from me, Melisa?" I ask.

"Everything!"

"What does that mean?" I say.

"It's self-explanatory."

"I mean, can you explain yourself?" I ask.

"The word needs no explanation," she says. "It explains itself."

"I guess we could go back and forth like this forever," I say.

"I guess we could," she says. "Or you could just admit that you no what I mean because I'm sure that you know what I mean."

"Everything is a big word, Melisa," I say.

"And I deserve everything because I have a big heart," she says. "I've never been the type of person that accepts less than what I'm worth."

"What are we talking about here?" I ask.

"I know what I'm talking about," she says. "The question is do you know what you're talking about?"

"You're a funny girl," I say.

"No, I'm a big girl that knows how to take care of herself," Melisa says.

"I don't have any arguments with that statement," I say. "You are schooled in the evil ways of the world."

"More importantly, I'm schooled at how God can redeem you of the evil ways of this world," Melisa says.

"Everything with you is about God," I say. "How does

God feel about you wanting to fuck me?"

"Don't try me, Fraser," Melisa says.

"What?" I ask.

"You know what," she says. "I ain't a fucking kid and ain't nothing about me slow."

"Who said I called you slow?"

"All you need to know is you can't fast talk me like you do everybody else," Melisa says. "You're my people's. You're my people's for real. But that ain't gonna stop me from cursing your ass out. Then I'm gonna kneel down and pray for you that same night before I go to sleep."

I don't respond. She has me speechless. What's a person supposed to say to a statement like that, anyway?

"To answer your question, though, God forgives all things," Melisa says. "So, if I want you and know that your limited mind only allows you to process physicality then I may decide to have you. And if it happens that way God will forgive me for that. At the end of the day, I'll no longer be a virgin..."

"Wait, you're a virgin?" I ask.

"Can I finish please?" she says. I nod my head. "As I was saying, if I give myself to you I'll no longer be a virgin but God will forgive me because in my heart he knows that I consider you to be my husband."

"That's deep," I say.

"Life is deep. Everything God put on this earth is deep."

"But, how could I be your husband when we've never been married?" I ask.

"You really do need to dig into your Bible," Melisa says. "The legal representation of marriage doesn't always jive with God's representation of marriage. If it did we wouldn't have so many divorces. Marriage is between a man and a woman and God, not between a man and a woman and the state."

"So, you're saying that the only way that you would have sex with me is if I told you that you could be mine?" I ask.

"What I'm saying is if I had sex with you then you wouldn't want to be anybody else's but mine," she says.

"How can you be so sure when you've never had sex before?" I ask. "You don't even know what you're doing."

"I know all I need to know," Melisa says. "And trust me, if I gave you this body you wouldn't want to go anywhere else. You can best believe that."

"I'm scared of you," I say.

Melisa breaks out in laughter.

"Boy, let me stop playing with you before you start thinking that I'm serious," she says.

"Oh, I know damned well that you're serious," I say.

"Then I guess that's for me to know and you to find out," Melisa says.

***

The next day Bongo is sitting in a chair at the Covington Street location even though it's early as hell when I get there.

"I went over the records for DC and Arlington this morning," he says. "Everything seems to be on point. I did have a couple of questions though. I highlighted stuff on the printouts. You can call Bijuani and Chi-town because I'm sure you'll know better than me what to ask me."

"Thanks, I'll look things over when I get settled in," I say.

"You know I love you to death, Fraser," Bongo says.

"I know you do…"

"Wait, hear me out," Bongo says. "I can't keep doing this, though. It's too stressful. I'm gonna mess around and give myself a heart attack."

"That's not my fault, though," I say. "You take the smallest shit way too seriously."

"But love is serious business, don't you know that?" Bongo asks. "When you truly love someone you're supposed to throw caution to the wind and totally dedicate yourself to them."

"Sometimes it hard for me to do that when I'm getting accused of doing all types of shit that I ain't even doing," I say.

"Do you want to buy me out?" Bongo asks.

"What? You're trippin'," I say.

Suddenly the seriousness of this discussion has taken on a whole new light to me.

"You can't handle me being around here all the time and I can't handle not being here when I don't know what you're doing with that Jezebel draped all over you all the time," Bongo says.

"Actually, you've got it all wrong," I say. "Melisa's favorite subject matter in conversations with me is religion. She's singing the same song to me that you are."

"I'm not dumb, Fraser," Bongo says. "I know love when I see it and I can see love in her eyes when she looks at you."

"Let's just say for a moment that you're right, don't I have something to say about all of this?" I ask. "Doesn't it take two to tangle and wouldn't I have to be a participant in whatever seamy things you have in your mind in order for them to come about?"

"Fraser, you're a whore, don't play me," Bongo says. "Granted, I love you but you were a whore when I met you and you're still a whore now."

"I haven't done shit since we started kicking it and that's the truth," I say. "You need to just stop trippin' and trust me."

"Maybe you haven't done anything, YET, but with a person like you it's just a matter of time," Bongo says. "I can't get angry at you, though, because it's in your blood. The best that I can do is protect myself."

"So, you want to sell the businesses?" I ask. "What happened to Urban Retro? I thought you were in this because we have our pulse on the Black community not just because you're feeling me."

"Honestly, I don't want to sell the business," Bongo says. "But I don't know what else to do."

"Since double-checking on your investment and being like a regional manager is not really in your blood I have a suggestion that I think may work," I say.

"At this point I think I'll be open to anything," Bongo says. "You know I love you too much to just throw everything we built away."

"Maybe we can space out Melisa's clients by giving her appointments at all three locations," I say. "Yes, the bulk of her clients will be seen on Covington since I really do depend on her for business reasons, plus you know how much Deja irks me, but if she checks on the other locations from time to time maybe you won't be so worried about her spending so much time around me. Besides, the business end of shit is much more in her blood than it is in yours."

"What if I don't want her all up in my business?" Bongo asks. "As you said, I have nothing to do with Covington but I have everything to do with the other locations we have."

"I'm just grasping for straws," I say. "I'm not trying to shove her down your throat. I'm just trying to make you feel more comfortable about the amount of time she has to interact with me. I mean, I've told you every way imaginable that nothing is going on with us but you still ain't trying to hear it. So, I just thought if I reduced the amount of time she was on Covington maybe that would reduce the amount of stress you're feeling from this situation."

"I really have been feeling sick," Bongo says. "I've been more than down in the dumps about everything."

"You'll be fine," I say. "Just give it a chance. How bout we just do it on a trial basis to see how things work out?'

"Ok, maybe you're right," Bongo says. "Tell her about the promotion but make sure that she knows it's only on a trial basis."

"I'll let her know as soon as she gets in," I say.

"Whew, I've just dodged another bullet," I think after he walks out.

All along I thought I was just playing Bongo. But, the scare I just had about him walking away from everything makes me wonder if I love him more than I'm admitting to myself.

Trying to process these feelings of connecting with another man isn't easy to do. You all know that I'm not gay. My story with sex with other men proves that it was always out of necessity or survival. I've never loved sweaty-ass balls niggas just like I've never loved them ho's.

Have I?

***

My mind is in a state of uncertainty when Melisa walks into the shop. She has on a pair of Bebe jeans, the ones with the butt cleavage, and a slinky silk shirt that has her six-packed stomach showing in its entirety.

"What, are you auditioning to be a hoochie today?" I ask her after giving her a hug and a kiss on the cheek.

"Don't start with me today, Fraser," she says. "I ain't in the fucking mood."

"hallelujah," I say, once again mocking her foul mouth and religious outlook.

She raises her middle finger to me in protest.

"Girl, the way you look today, I don't know," I say while rubbing on my chin like I'm checking her out.

She plays right along by switching hard as she walks away.

When she comes back from putting her things away I look at her with a smile on my face. I must be trippin' cause I can't take my eyes off of you.

"What? Fraser, damn!" she says. "You're spooking me out right now."

"Oh, I have some good news for you, that's all," I say, knowing that wasn't the only reason I was staring at her.

"Well, spit it out," she says.

"You know how you're always helping me when I'm looking over the reports from DC and Arlington?" I say.

"How can I forget?" she replies before saying, "Wait a minute. Is this good news for me or good news for you?"

"Will you let me finish saying what I'm saying, woman? Damn. It's good news for both of us," I say, sounding exasperated.

"Sorry, my brother, you can proceed," she says while pumping her fists.

"Thank you," I say. "Now, like I was saying before I was so rudely interrupted. Ah hmm. Bongo has been falling off too much as far as staying on top of Bijuani and Chi-town."

"That's an understatement," she says.

I cut my eyes at her evilly and she puts her head down,

breaking away from my stare. Normally she won't back down but she knows she's wrong to keep interrupting me.

"Anyway," I say. "I want you to take between ten to twenty hours a week in appointments at those locations. I need you to be my eyes and ears. I need you to be my Assistant Manager. And I'm not talking about you being an Assistant Manager in DC or Arlington. I'm talking about them answering to you and you answering to me."

"Are you serious?" she says, smiling. "Wait! What is Bongo gonna say about this?"

"He's with it," I say. She looks at me with suspicious eyes. "Well, to be honest at first he wasn't with it so I presented my argument to him about you. Emotions aside, he knows as well as I knows that you're the best fit. That's why he agreed with me. Well, he agreed enough to tell me he'd let you do it on a temporary basis. Basically, this is your time to shine. If you fuck it up you have nobody to blame but yourself."

Melisa scans my face long enough to see that I'm dead serious about what I'm saying. Once she's convinced that I'm not joking, she jumps into my arms squeezing me like she's trying to give me a bear hug.

"Wow, Fraser, this is wonderful," she says.

"You deserve it," I say, trying to make it seem like it's nothing.

"I appreciate you so much for looking out for me," she says, looking me squarely in the eyes.

Her greenish, gray eyes look amazing this close up. I can't understand for the life of me how she can be single.

"Seriously, Fraser," she says, continuing. "From day one you've taken me under your wing. You've been a mentor, a friend... an instructor. I honestly don't know what I'd do without you."

I tell myself that I shouldn't be caught up with her inside this tender moment. I tell myself that I have to look away from those eyes, quickly, before it gets to be too late. But honestly, I'm stuck. It feels like her eyes are quicksand and mine are slowing sinking under their power.

Without giving me the chance to continue pondering escaping from her grasp, Melisa gives me the sweetest, most tender, most passionate kiss I've had in a very long time.

Her lips are the smoothest things that I've ever felt. Her tongue tastes like its made of magic. I'm exploring her mouth as if my life depends on it.

I can't relinquish the opportunity to take advantage of the chance to squeeze her plump ass. I've been admiring it for a long time so when I start rubbing on it with both hands, I feel like a kid in a candy store. My heart is smiling. Truthfully, I didn't even know that I could feel this good. The best way to describe it is to say that I'm so at peace right now.

"You really know how to thank a nigga," I say when we finally take a break from kissing.

"Oh, but I'm not done thanking you," she says seductively.

"Do you really wanna go there, Melisa?" I ask. "I mean, now that I know that you're a virgin. I'm wondering if you really think it's best for me to be your first."

"But, you won't be my first," she says.

I give her a look that says I can't understand why she would lie to me.

"What I mean is you're not only my first," she says correcting herself. "I consider you to be my first… my last… my everything."

Maybe her words seem corny if you consider the fact that they're lyrics to a song made famous by Isaac Hayes in the seventies.

But, coming out of her mouth they sounded so sexy, so sensual, and so true.

This time, I bring my face to hers and once again explore her lips and her mouth while squeezing on her ass. To say that my dick is hard as a rock is beyond being an understatement.

"You know that some would consider this to be sexual harassment?" Melisa says to me, breaking her words up through alternating with kisses.

"Yeah, it could be conceived as a conflict of interest," I say, joining her in her game. "But, remember, you kissed me first."

"So what, you kissed me last," she says.

Suddenly she breaks away from me looking at me with wild eyes.

"I can't believe we're doing this here," she says. "Especially if this is the day you're going to announce to everyone that I'm your Assistant Manager." She paused for a second then grabs my hand before continuing to speak. "Come on. I think that we should at least take this to the hair braiding room."

"Hell no," I say, feeling like that's beneath us. Actually I think it's beneath her not me. "You're worth too much for that. I would never fuck you in some back room of a barbershop. At least not the first time. It should be magical. I promise you I want you. But I want it to be magical more."

I cannot even believe the words that just came out of my mouth. Honestly, I'm wondering if someone has invaded my body and taken over my vocal cords.

"That's why I know I was right to choose you to love," Melisa says. "Sure, you're rough around the edges with everybody else, but with me you're like the most adorable damned teddy bear there is. And I know you're gonna make our lovemaking special. It'll be as magical as you're saying it's gonna be. But, for now, I need you to take me upstairs and fuck me like I'm your whore. I wanna be that for you. I wanna be everything to you just like I feel like you're everything to me. Let's just say you owe me a romantic, magical lovemaking experience. But right now I need to give myself to a man for the very first time. My body is calling you, Fraser. Now it's up to you to show me that you're listening."

I can't tell you how glad that I am that Melisa saved me from my own stupidity. Hell yeah I want to be with her, right here and right now.

Later I think I'll have to examine what was going on inside of my head to make me choose honor and respect over getting a prime piece of ass. But, for now, my dick is telling me that it needs fulfillment. You tell me which head you think I'm gonna listen to.

CHAPTER EIGHT

Conflict of Interest

Melisa is just the second woman that I've given oral sex to. And I have to tell you, her pussy tastes amazing.

I'm sucking on her pussy lips, kissing them, adoring them, and I'm taking every opportunity to lick up every once of the creaminess that oozes out of her secret garden. She wants to return the favor but I don't want that from her. If she's never had sex I'm sure that she can't really no how to suck a dick. At this point I don't want a single negative thought in my head about Melisa.

Another reason that she can't suck my dick is I have no intentions of making her a victim. Don't think that I'm getting soft because I'm not. Honestly, I can't explain it so don't fucking push me. This is my moment so let me enjoy it. I've been waiting for this for such a long time.

"You don't need that," Melisa says as I pull the Magnum out of my wallet. "I really want to feel you."

"And you will feel me, Baby," I say. "But we both know that this is best." She looks at me with pleading eyes. I can tell how bad she really wants the dick. "Please don't fight me over this. We have our entire life to take the condom off. But today let's do it the right way."

The passionate kiss that Melisa plants on my mouth tells me that my words won her over. That's the first time that my game actually surpassed her game. Maybe it's just because she wants wholeheartedly to believe that I mean everything that I'm saying.

For my part, I think I mean everything. Even if I don't understand my actions or my words I feel like I'm being sincere.

Melisa feels like a tight faucet of overflowing water when I stick my dick inside of her.

She yelps. I know that she can't be lying about this being the first time that she's felt the pleasure & pain mixture that many women have come to know as sex.

I feel her hymen bursting around my dick as she grabs my back, digging her nails inside of me.

Her passion and intensity is evident. I understand what she means when she said she's giving herself to me.

Melisa's face has the expression of a woman that has totally given in to her cause. She's locked into her position and no one in the world is going to move her off of her spot.

Based on the tears that's falling from Melisa's eyes, I know that this encounter is far from a tryst. I honestly feel like this is where I belong but judging from my past experiences and fickle mind, I wonder if this can of worms that I've just opened is going to blow up in my face.

Just moments ago I was telling myself that I was refusing to admit that I had real feelings for another man. Now, I'm in the midst of the greatest feelings I may have ever felt in my life.

Diane must be smiling down on me because I could never make those statements about another woman if I didn't feel that she's cool with it. Knowing Diane, she would want me to be happy even though I ruined her life.

The thought of Diane and the tears in Melisa's eyes combine to overpower me. Before long, we're crying together as we're making love.

Maybe my tears aren't totally legitimate since they aren't all about Melisa, but she's moved by them just the same.

In my mind I'm noticing scented candles and rose petals. Soft music and even softer lights. And though my thoughts don't describe our current reality, the moment is still magical to me. I feel like I'm swimming in a cloud.

***

"Come here, Fraser," Bongo says, sounding like he's irked-for what now I don't know.

I follow him outside, wondering why he's chosen to leave the salon to talk. It's not like he can't see how busy I am.

"I'm tired of you fucking playing me, Fraser," he yells.

"Now what the hell are you talking about?" I ask.

"You're supposed to be telling Melisa she can be Assistant Manager on a trial basis, not helping her celebrate," Bongo snaps.

"What the hell are you talking about?" I say. "I haven't even told her yet. You're confusing me right now."

Bongo inches closer to me.

"I know a bitch when I smell one," he says suspiciously. "And it's her scent that's all over you."

"Wow, you're really losing it," I say. "I don't know where you come up with some of this stuff."

"I would say from right here," he says as he picks a piece of Melisa's hair from off of my shirt. "But that's too obvious. It's too easy. The harder thing is for you to step up to the plate and try to be honest for once in your life. Just tell me that you did it but you won't let it happen again."

"Now you're telling me what I did, come on now," I say. "You can't tell me what I did."

"Ok, so you don't wanna do this the easy way; let's do this another way," Bongo says, angrily as he turns to walk to the salon door.

Curiously, I follow him, trying to figure out what he's up to.

"Melisa, we need to talk to you out here," Bongo says, not even putting forth an effort to take the edge off his voice."

"Ok, give me one second," Melisa says. "I need to finish one thing with my client before I can walk away."

"Well, we don't really have a second but do what you can do," Bongo says, letting the door shut before Melisa has a chance to answer him."

"What are you doing?" I ask.

"I'm handling this now," Bongo spits. "You had your chance."

I shake my head while looking him up and down. I really do hope that he gets control of his emotions.

"What's going on?" Melisa asks when she walks outside.

"The bottom line is I have too much to lose to have you fucking my partner when you're supposed to be remaining objection about business," Bongo says.

"Excuse me," Melisa says. "Fraser, what did you tell him?" she asks, turning to me.

"He didn't have to tell me anything," Bongo replies. "It's written all over your face. Just like your funky scent is oozing out of his trifling ass pores."

"Who the hell are you calling funky?" Melisa asks, balling up her fists. "And you're not really sounding like a partner right now. Your conversation is sounding like it's on some other stuff."

"Don't you worry about my conversation," Bongo snaps. "All you need to worry about is being the best damned Assistant Manager that you can be. Congratulations on your promotion but keep your fucking hands off my partner. I'm not gonna let neither one of y'all hormones drag my investment into the dumps."

Bongo stomps away and Melisa looks at me curiously.

I don't say anything because I'm at a loss for words.

"What was that about?" she asks.

"Congratulations on your promotion," I respond. "Don't say anything yet, though. I wanna be the one that tells the rest of the staff."

I walk inside with my mind clouded. I'm trying to figure everything out and process the events of the day thus far.

"What the fuck am I supposed to do now?" I think.

I'm not exactly sure but I know I'd better come up with something quick, fast, and in a hurry.

***

"Melisa, damn, can you pay attention," I say when I see someone sitting in a chair waiting to have her hair washed. It's only been two minutes but judging from the bass in my voice you'd think it had been two hours.

I can't figure out if the way that I've been treating Melisa today since after

Bongo left is a defense mechanism to show the staff that I'm not giving her special treatment prior to announcing her promotion or if I'm trying to show her that she doesn't have the power over me that she thinks she has. I wonder if I feel I've made a terrible mistake.

The fact of the matter is that Bongo's my bread and butter. No one can doubt how pissed he thinking that I fucked Melisa's today. I have to come up with a way to pick up the pieces.

***

It's Saturday night and I'm glad that one horrendous week of doing hair is over.

The conundrum that matches so many opposing forces that are not in harmony with each other has basically given me a headache.

I've been cold as shit to Melisa since the conflict with Bongo about her giving me her virginity. Every time that I want to grab her and kiss her I've opted to yell at her instead.

How can I balance love with my survival of the fittest type instincts? How can I decide to build with someone when there's someone else that's ready, willing, and capable to build me up and give me any and everything that I damn well desire in this world?

I love Bongo dearly. But I've come to the realization that I truly believe I could fall in love with Melisa like I've never done before.

Could I live with myself if I kept up my façade with him? We all know that I'm highly capable of that.

But, I am concerned by the fact that Bongo lives on an emotional roller coaster twenty-four hours a day and seven days a week. He's the epitome of a drama king. And trust me, if you think a woman can be a drama queen, you haven't seen nothing until you've come across a gay male with the same type of mental disposition.

The lights are all out when I walk into the house on Conway. I'm baffled by the fact that Bongo's not even home.

In a way, though, I'm glad. That will give me a chance to relax my mind a little without him badgering me.

"How was work today? How did Melisa do with DC and Arlington?"

I can hear him asking me a bunch of meaningless questions now while not asking the one that he really wants to ask, "How much time was that Melisa bitch all up in your face today?"

Seemingly almost on cue, I hear Bongo sticking his key in the door. It's like I thought about him and here he is. Thankfully, he's quiet when he comes in the house. Besides speaking, he doesn't have much to say at all.

Originally, I'm happy. This will be the first quiet night I've had in a long time. Yet, after a while, it occurs to me that Bongo isn't acting like himself. I have to make sure that his attitude has nothing to do with me. I'm not the type of person that makes it a habit to bite the hand that feeds me.

"Bongo, what's up with you?" I say. "Why are you so quiet?"

"I just have a lot on my mind," he says. "There's no need for both of us to have the weight of the world on our shoulders."

"I'm not trying to be funny but normally if you have a

splinter in your hand you'll wake me up at three o'clock in the morning to tell me," I say. "If you're not willing to share it must be something deep."

"You don't know the half of it," Bongo says.

"Ok. Try me," I respond.

"I think that you should get yourself right with God while you have a chance," Bongo says.

"Wait a minute, " I say. "You've never had a problem with telling me you wanted to drag me to your father's church before. And you barely go. What's this really about?"

"I'm just saying that I'm trying to get myself on the right track," he says. "If you help me then it will be that much easier. You should go with me every Sunday. If you agree to go there's no way that I'd keep myself home."

"Why now, Bongo?" I ask. "There's something going on that you're not telling me."

"Is there ever really a right time to get right with God?" Bongo asks. "I thought any time would be considered to be the right time for that."

"Bongo, don't bullshit a bullshitter," I say. "Just tell me what the fuck is going on."

"I ruined your life," he says, breaking out in tears.

Before I know it, he's running up the stairs two at a time.

"What in the world is wrong with this crazy motherfucker?" I say under my breath.

Against my better judgment, I follow him up the stairs and go into his room. He's laying across the bed sobbing uncontrollably.

"Bongo, this isn't funny anymore," I say. "What the fuck is going on with you?"

It takes him a moment to compose himself. When he does, he sits up in the bed and crosses his arms around his knees, resting his head on the back of his hands.

"I have to tell you something, Fraser," he says. "And there's nothing funny about it. It's actually very, very serious."

At that point I really was getting worried. I wondered what it could possibly be.

"You need to go and get yourself tested," Bongo says. The tears return to his eyes but he isn't out of control like he was before. "I made sure to verify with the doctor that just because I'm where I am it doesn't mean that you have to be there as well."

"Bongo, what the fuck are you talking about?" I ask. At this point he has me confused.

"You know how I've been feeling drained for a while, having no energy?" he says.

I shake my head. Honestly, I thought it was because he

didn't like me being around Melisa.

"There's no other way to say it but to say it," Bongo commences slowly. "I have full blown AIDS and you have to get yourself checked out like yesterday. This is nothing to play around with, Fraser."

I slump down on the bed. A million thoughts run through my head.

"You're kidding me, Bongo," I say.

"I wish I was," he responds. "Trust me I wish I was."

I sit silently. I have no words to say. Actually, I don't think that I have anything worthwhile to add to this discussion.

"I know you want to kill me," Bongo says. "I mean, I did put you at risk."

"I'm not even thinking about it like that," I say, calmly. "I know if I am at risk it's not something that you did intentionally."

I'm amazed at how calm I am regarding the situation. I'm also proud of myself for being able to deflect any thought that may come into my head that makes me look the slightest bit guilty.

I'm a picture of composure. I doubt very seriously that there's anything that Bongo could say to me at this point to break me down.

He hands me a piece of paper that has a list of names, addresses, and phone numbers on it.

"What's this?" I ask.

"Not that it matters now but I'd really like to know who did this to me," he says. "Well, actually who did this to us."

"Come again," I say.

" I want you to help me find out who gave this to me," he says. "I found my soul mate in you but due to someone's recklessness I won't be able to grow old with you as I planned. Please tell me that you'll help me. I know you spend a lot of time at the salon but there has to be a way to balance the two things."

So basically Bongo wants me to look for myself although I'm not on his list so I won't really be looking for myself. I guess I spoke too quickly when I said that there's nothing that Bongo could say to unnerve me.

I get up off the bed and break out of the room as quickly as I possibly can.

"Fraser… Fraser," I hear Bongo calling me but he doesn't run behind me like he normally would do when I walk out on him.

I guess he knows I need my space right now.

When I get back to Bongo's he's sleeping in his bed cuddled up with Patch. He had to think that I wouldn't be returning or he wouldn't have allowed Patch to be in the bed with him. I've told him repeatedly in no uncertain terms how much I hate that mutt of his.

I decide not to bother him and sneak out. It was probably a bad idea to come back here bothering him in the first place.

I drive back to my own place and sit in the bed staring at the walls. There won't be much sleep for me tonight. Counting sheep just won't cut it with all the shit that I have on my mind.

I decide to call the only person that I've really been having discussions like this with. Though, at this point, I'm not sure if she'll talk to me judging by the way that I've been treating her lately.

"Fraser, what's wrong?" Melisa asks. "It's almost three o'clock in the morning."

"I know and I'm sorry for waking you," I say. "I didn't really know who else to talk to."

"Well, I already knew that you had some huge weights on your shoulders," she says. "You haven't exactly been acting like Miss Congeniality."

"I know and I'm sorry," I say. "But I can't explain it right now. I promise to let you know when it's time."

"You don't owe me anything, Fraser," Melisa says. "I

only want your heart and you've already given me that whether you know it or not. I'd consider myself to be such a bad person if I wasn't there for you just because you've been acting grumpy. I hope you know that I'm bigger than that."

"That you are," I say. "That's why I appreciate you so much. You came out of nowhere and became the unconditional friend to me that I didn't think existed anymore in this world."

Suddenly I think of Miss Victim Number Two. Besides her, no one ever treated me the way Melisa has treated me since the first day I got to know her. I loved Diane to death but lord knows she had her faults. It's funny how you never miss your water until the well runs dry.

"So, are you gonna tell me what this is all about?" Melisa asks. "It is kind of late right now."

"You know what? I'm being selfish," I say. "I promise to tell you tomorrow morning at the shop. There's no way in the world you'll be able to get back to sleep if I lay this on you tonight. One of us has to have the energy to tame the savage beasts we have on our staff."

"I really don't mind but if you think that's best then ok," Melisa says. "Just try to be strong. And I know you don't do it all the time. You may not do it ever. But kneel down and pray to God for strength tonight. If you call out to him he'll come."

"I'll keep that in mind," I say. Melisa's silence tells me that she doesn't believe me. "For real I may just do that tonight. I promise you I'll never lie to you ever."

"Ok, Baby, I love you," Melisa says.

Silently, I hang up the phone.

CHAPTER NINE

Chasing One's Own Tail

The wet streets lead me to believe that the rain has washed away all the impurities in the world over night. I wonder if the miniscule amounts of drizzle that remain are aimed at purifying me.

I'm feeling anxious about what I'll say when Melisa comes in. I struggle over and over in my head with the fact that I told her I'd never lie to her on the phone.

I promise you that's something I've never told anyone before. Hell, I've never even thought it.

Could I possibly have meant I'd be totally truthful with her? I never thought that I was built like that but is it conceivable that even a piece of shit like me can change my trifling ways?

I don't fight Melisa when she greets me with a steamy, passionate kiss. This is the first time since our Sexcapade and, believe me, her lips still taste good.

"So, I hope you slept good last night," Melisa says. I know she's trying her best to break the ice.

"Why do you like me, Melisa?" I ask. "You say you chose me but what would make you want to?"

"Is that what you called me to talk about at three o'clock in the morning?" she asks.

"Not really but I'm just curious."

"Well, all I can say is I chose you because I felt like I was drawn to you," she says. "When someone is meant for you, you just know."

"That's not the type of statement I'd normally understand but I think I know where you're coming from," I say.

"Sometimes fate operates without any rhyme or reason."

I am curious about where Melisa came from. What made her walk into HBS when she was exactly what we needed?

Truth be told, I haven't exactly been an example of compassion during my life. Why was I sent such an excellent example of how a person is supposed to treat other people? You would think that the person that showed up at HBS instead of Melisa would have been a piece of shit like me. That's what I've dished out. I thought that's what I was supposed to take.

"Boy, what is on your mind?" Melisa asks.

"Do you know that you're the only person that I ever allow to call me boy?" I ask. "You've seen me dig in people's shit for a lot less."

"Don't make me blush, please," Melisa says. "I love you even more when you tell me that you extend the boundaries of your universe for me. It makes me feel more special than you'll ever know."

"You have to promise me that you won't tell this to anyone," I say.

I feel like I have to get down to it. I've bullshitted around long enough.

"I promise, Baby," she says. "I would never compromise your faith in me. Nothing you ever say to me in confidence will ever leave these lips."

"Good, because if it did then Bongo would kill you," I say.

"What does he have to do with this?" Melisa asks.

"Everything," I respond.

"Now I'm confused," she says.

Her face tells me that she isn't lying.

"Basically, Bongo asked me for my help with something," I say. "And I want you to help me. Honestly, I have to help him. But, I doubt very seriously if I can do this by myself. I may be able to pull it off, though, if you're in my corner."

"I'm always gonna be in your corner, Babe, but right now I'm clueless about what you're trying to say," Melisa responds.

"Bongo has full blown AIDS," I say, searching her face to see if her expression cracks.

"Wow. That's big," she says. "I really don't know how to respond to that other than saying it's kind of foul for you to tell me that man's personal business. People's health records and status are supposed to be one of the most sacred things about someone nowadays."

"I know and I feel like shit about it," I say. "But, I'm being honest when I say I won't be able to do what he asked me to do without you supporting me."

"What exactly does he want you to do?" Melisa asks. "It's not like you're a doctor or miracle worker."

"That's funny," I say. "Basically, he gave me a list of names of past sexual partners. He wants me to help him find out who infected him with the disease. He looked me straight in my eyes and said that he'd like to know that before he dies."

"This is even more major than I thought," Melisa says.

"But I am curious about one thing. You do know that Bongo can't stand my guts, right?"

"Believe me, I'm aware of that," I say. "But, that doesn't matter since you promised to exercise discretion. I'm one-hundred percent confident that if you tell me something you mean it."

"It's good to know that you know me," Melisa says. She extends her hands to me. "So, lets shake on the fact that we're partners in this endeavor as well." I grab her hand and shake it. "I'll follow you to the end of the earth, Fraser. If you need me I'm there."

***

For months Melisa and I work our way down the names on our list while Bongo attacks his list by himself.

One by one we cross off name after name. In my heart I know we're racing against time.

If there really is a God and if that God has a heart he will allow Bongo to die before he gets to the bottom of his quest. His obsession with knowing can't be too healthy. Plus if he really knew the truth, that it itself would kill him off well before it's time.

Bongo is teary-eyed sitting on the living room couch when I get to his house. Once again he's hugging Patch like he's a teddy bear that a young child's grandmother gave him right before she passed away.

I know that some of anything could be on Bongo's mind. He's emotional and for good reason.

I stare at him and think of the words that the doctor told me in Trenton. I wouldn't have dared to go get myself checked out in a neighborhood where anyone had known me back when I thought I was at risk.

"No two people's genetic make-ups are alike, Mr. Fraser," she had said. "Your HIV has been in a dormant state much longer than most. That doesn't mean that you can't infect someone else, though, so definitely exercise safe sex. Believe me; anyone else that has had the disease as long as you had it without treatment would have already progressed to the next step. They would die ten times faster than you'll even get a cough."

Bongo had the perfect life. He was adopted into the money and he had the world at his feet. Unlike me who's had to scheme and scratch for every dime I ever had, Bongo's opportunities in life were endless.

I suddenly feel sorry for him for being so weak. He threw caution to the wind while coming at me. He didn't question anything. Whatever I told him he believed me.

Granted, I have to admit that everyone in the world isn't cruel but that doesn't stop me from being a cynic.

I will look at each and every person sideways when I meet them before I give them an inch. You have to prove to me that your major purpose in life isn't to take me down before I even begin to take anything that you say seriously.

I would be a fool to take something someone said as a fact just because they wanted me to. No one's mouth is a prayer book. Knowing myself as well as I do helped me to learn that.

"This shit is so much harder than "I thought it would be, Fraser," Bongo says with speech broken by his cries. "I always considered myself to be prepared for death. I shouldn't be letting this weigh me down as much as it is."

"You're being human, that's all," I say. "I don't fault you one bit. And I definitely think it's normal for you not to be strong. I would consider you to be acting fake if you were sticking your chest out like this isn't phasing you."

"I'm so glad that I didn't give this to you," Bongo says. I remember that I paid a crooked doctor to give me a letter saying that my HIV test came back clean despite him never testing me in the first place. It's a shame that you can buy anything in this world if you have enough money. Even a doctor's Hippocratic oath can be broken.

Bongo squeezes Patch harder. In response, Patch licks Bongo in his face with love.

"Promise me that you'll take care of Patch," Bongo says. "I know you aren't exactly his biggest fan but you do know how much he means to me. I want to make sure that Patch has a loving home."

"I promise you that he will," I say.

I didn't exactly lie. It may not be me but I'll make sure for Bongo that someone looks out for his mutt. That's the least that I could do.

CHAPTER TEN

The Beginning of the End

It's amazing to see the effect that AIDS is having on Bongo. His skin has gotten at least two shades darker. But that doesn't help to hide the dark patches that you can see underneath of his eyes.

He looks twenty years older than he actually is. If you haven't seen Bongo in years, when you look at him now you'd think someone was lying to you when he told you that Bongo's the same person.

His looks, though, are only half of his problem. His coughs have become deep and troubling. It sounds like his insides will come up each and every time you here him trying to clear out his air passages. I'd be lying to you if I told you that Bongo was having a quiet and peaceful death.

***

It seems like an eternity since the last time I've been inside of the First Abyssian Baptist Church.

I'm spooked by the fact that the last time I was here it was because Bongo was burying his dad. Today I'm burying Bongo.

This is the first time that I've ever been this close to the consequences of my actions. Seeing everyone in the edifice overtaken with tears and sadness doesn't make me feel good at all.

I wonder what they would do to me if they knew that it was me that gave him the deadly disease that took him out of the game. I wonder if they'd allow me to make it out of this church alive.

I take comfort in the fact that Bongo found the answers that he was looking for prior to his death. No matter how obsessed he was with succeeding in his quest, I'm certain that things worked out for the best.

Organizing Bongo's things is kind of hard for me. I feel a little guilty because none of this would be happening if it weren't for me.

I've pondered for days what my intentions were with Bongo. I knew he had money, I knew he had clout, but I don't feel like I intentionally planned to make him become a victim from the onset like I've done with so many of the female sexpots that I conquered.

I'm glad that Bongo made it clear that he wanted most of his worldly possessions to go to a plethora of different charities. At least now I won't have to deal with a bunch of people I don't even know staking their claim to items that they probably don't deserve anyway.

Bongo's cleanliness is a confirmation of the fact that he's a truly gay male. Going through his things and separating what she'd be donated to charity from what should be shredded to protect his legacy is turning to be a cinch. I'm not sure how something on the desk in his private study catches my attention but it does. My curiosity gets even more sparked when I see my name scribbled on a piece of paper that coming out the side of a folder.

Immediately I pick up the folder. I gasp when I look at its contents.

Apparently it's a file given to Bongo from Thomas Sterner Private Investigations. Since everything inside of it is about me it's clear that Bongo did a background check on me to find out something about the person he planned to give his heart to.

"So, Bongo wasn't as weak or dumb as I thought," I think. "He protected his interest after all."

I peruse page after page of things that I never would have imagined Bongo knew about me. The only conclusion I can come up with is that his love for me was so deep that it rose above all of my imperfections.

Honestly, I've never figured out how someone could love another so deeply. I certainly haven't and doubt serious if I ever will.

When I see an envelope from the Sing Sing Correctional Facility in New York I immediately get nervous. Like I thought, Freddie's is the name that I see written in the return address area.

"What the fuck is Bongo doing with a letter from Freddie?" I ask myself, knowing full well that I'm about to find out for sure.

Mr. Long

Thank you very much for agreeing to hear me out. I was surprised when someone reached out to me. No one knows better than me how calculative Michael Fraser is when he comes up with a plan to bleed someone dry like a turnip. He isolated us from anyone from on the East Coast that would know our stories while we were in Baltimore. Prior to hearing from Mr. Sterner I was convinced that he was going to get away totally with what he did.

You're a grown man and you have to make your own decisions. But if you're looking for advice I can tell you that Michael doesn't love you. I'm not sure he's even capable of love.

Granted, he's a very good pretender. When you're with him you think that you've grown on him just as much as he's grown on you.

If you knew like I knew, you wouldn't believe it. Look inside the glove compartment of the Infiniti he's driving and you'll see my name on the title. I loved that car more than anything. I guess him taking it from me was his final stamp of defiance that would prove to me that in Michael's world you get punished for loving anything half as much as you love him. Try that and he'll take it away from you.

I know you must have money or you wouldn't be able to hire a private investigator. The other clue of your fortune is I'm positive that Michael wouldn't be with you if you were broke. You have to bring something to his table not appear like you'll be the type of person that takes things away.

Surprisingly, I harbor no ill feelings towards Michael. By the way, you're probably confused by my use of his government name. He told me when we got to Baltimore to just call him Fraser. After a while, people were thinking that was his first name, not his last. Or maybe they thought that he only had one name like Madonna. Whatever the case, no one ever asked him what his first name was so he achieved the ability to hide his full name from people so no one could check him out.

As far as ill feelings, I can't blame it on Michael for my being locked up. Even if he hadn't called my parole officer my fugitive status would have caught up with me eventually. I should have maxed out on all of my time like Michael did prior to relocating. The lesson I've learned from this entire ordeal is you can't run from your past. I thought I'd finally made something of myself. Being partners with Michael in a venture I invested most of my life savings on may have seemed scary in the beginning. But I have to hand it to him. He made HBS work. We were making a killing before my parole officer had me expedited back to New York. Now the entire business is his.

If you think about it, Michael is a brilliant man. He invested two-thousand-dollars into HBS compared to my twenty thousand. Now he's the sole owner of a business that's approaching a quarter million in revenues. If that's not a testament to Don King's statement, "Only in America," I don't know what is.

Well, Mr. Long, I think I'll go since now I'm rambling. But, before I do, I need you to know that you shouldn't trust Michael Fraser no further than you can see him. If you do try to trust him, your world will come tumbling down just as quickly as mine did. You'll find out that it's only a matter of time.

Peace and blessings,

Freddie Fleming, Michael Fraser's ex-lover and business partner

I can't believe that Bongo knew all about me. He must've been trying to get me to admit certain things about myself. I wonder if my dealings with Michael are all he knew about. There isn't anything in the file to say he found out about my HIV status but I'm still not sure.

Immediately, I wonder if he's spoken to anyone else about me. I wonder if he took my secrets to his grave with me or told half of Baltimore, determined that he was gonna make sure that my past caught up to me.

"Ok, Fraser, focus," I say to myself.

I know I need to get myself together prior to going in to the shop. I haven't been spending that much time there since Bongo's death but today I have to go in to square the money away. Yes, Melisa's been a godsend to me but there's no one in the world that I trust more with my money than myself.

I gather up Patch's broken down bones and carry him out to the car with me. I can't tell you how much I hate that I have to care for this mutt. I wonder if I'm gonna be able to follow through with that request that Bongo asked me to do before he died.

The salon is a lot quieter than I thought it would be when I get there. I don't know how she did it but Melisa held her own with the barbers.

Speaking of the barbers, I head by them as I walk toward the hair braiding room. Patch is following me. I carried him up the stairs but don't want the mutt to get in the habit of thinking I'm gonna be his best friend like Bongo was.

"Wait! Wait!" I hear Rick's voice yelling from the barbershop. "Where you think you going with that fucking mutt. Look at him y'all. He's fucking hobbling."

"I know, man, I think his leg must be broke," Stacks says, adding his two cents to the bashing. I'm sure he's happy to join in on ridiculing me since I pulled his card about tricking with Deja in my shop. That seems like the type of dog somebody like Antwan on in living color would be walking. Yo, Fraser, why don't you get that motherfucker a crutch or something?"

I can't believe I've become the butt of some joke over a dog I can't even stand. I've had a bad enough day already learning that Bongo knew shit about me that I wasn't aware of. I'm not about to let this shit going on.

But go on it did. It's been hours and these bastards are still talking shit to me about this damned dog. I know in my mind that I've had enough.

When I leave here with this dog I'm never bringing him back again. And don't even think I'd consider taking him home with me. I'm getting rid of this mutt as quick as I possibly can.

I ask Melisa to join me upstairs in the hair braiding room so that we can talk. It's been a long day for me and although I've been keeping my distance from her, right now I can use her friendship.

"What's going on, boss?" she asks.

I can tell she's trying to be funny.

"Please, not today," I say. "I don't need the day to get any worse."

"I just don't know how to take you, that's all," she says.

"But, I am concerned about you. I can't hide that. Tell me what's going on."

"What's going on is I can't believe that Bongo had a private investigator looking into me before he died," I say, matter-of-factly.

"Why would he want to do that?" Melisa asks.

"Your guess is as good as mine," I say, lying. "Maybe he didn't trust me as much as I thought he did with this business deal."

"You shouldn't kick dirt on a dead man's grave," Melisa says. "Yeah we had our differences but I won't drudge all of that up right now. Just be thankful that he had you checked out and you came away clean as a whistle. I'm sure he would have been quick to curse you out if he found out anything damaging. You know how emotional the man was."

"Yeah, maybe you're right," I say.

I seriously hadn't thought about things in the way Melisa just kicked them to me. I've been too busy thinking that Bongo was being sneaky. The fact of the matter is I'm the champion of walking around with my Poker face on. I need to stop letting people think that anything is getting to me.

Melisa gives me a hug as we finish up our discussion. Her body feels so good against mine.

But, I have to be strong. I don't feel like I'm out of the woodworks yet. My number one concern is being careful. After that, I need to get back my swagger. Getting rid of this mutt when I leave here will do a lot to put me on that path.

CHAPTER ELEVEN

A Dog's Life

I head in the direction of Conway as soon as I leave the shop. I'm looking for a homeless guy that's nicknamed Thrifty due to the fact that he'll fix the transmission on your car, paint your entire house, or shovels your snow for hours after a blizzard dumps three feet of it on your stairs and in your driveway all for the incredibly low price of five dollars.

Honestly, I'm not sure what he charges though I know it's not much. More importantly, I saw how Thrifty was interacting with Patch one time Bongo got Thrifty to do the landscaping in his yard. I know he loves the dog so at least I won't be reneging on my promise to make sure that Patch is raised by someone that will give him a good home.

I know what you're thinking. Thrifty won't be able to give him extravagant breeders and handcrafted dog houses, but just like Luther sang about a house not being a home if love doesn't live there, none of that stuff will matter to Patch as long as he has a companion that pays attention to him.

I circle the area where the shameless, snooty people hire downtrodden guys like Thrifty to do hundreds or thousands of dollars worth of work for next to nothing. I'm sure that if I just keep it up I'll get lucky.

Sure enough, I peep Thrifty raking leaves in this huge house located inside one of the pricier cull de sac's in the neighborhood. Happily, I drive toward him. I can't wait to get Patch off my hands.

Pulling up in front of the house where Thrifty is raking leaves, I put the car in neutral and get out. Thrifty looks towards me as if he's wondering who I am. I'm not sure if he remembers me from Bongo so I open my door to get out then open the back door to pick up Patch. No sooner than I close the door Thrifty notices the raggedy looking dog I'm about to get rid of and yells his name.

"Patch… Hey little fella," Thrifty says as Patch barks hysterically upon seeing him and recognizing his voice.

I get right to the point.

"I have some bad news for you," I say. "Bongo passed away."

"Damn, that's a shame," Thrifty says.

I can't tell if he's seriously moved by Bongo's death or

if he's just upset that he's lost one of his most reliable hookups for handyman jobs.

"That's not all," I say. "Before he died, he made me promise that Patch would be taken care of by someone that loves him. I remembered how close the two of you were and was hoping that you would look after Patch."

"I love Patch," Thrifty says. "But things have been kind of rough lately. I can barely feed myself. I don't want Patch to have to experience a growling stomach like me when he's used to eating well every day."

"Say no more," I say quickly.

I reach in my pocket and pull out a hundred dollar bill.

"Thanks for the gesture," Thrifty says. "And I'm not trying to be a pain in the ass but look at me. What would you say if I came into your business and gave you a big bill like that?"

"I see your point," I say.

I dig into my pocket and pull out six twenty-dollar-bills. I hand them to Thrifty like we're doing a drug deal. Getting rid of Patch feels so close that I can taste it.

"Are you sure you want to let go of Patch?" Thrifty asks. "He's a great dog."

"I think it will be best," I say. "It's obvious that he'd rather be with you than me. Look how his face lit up and how he started barking when he saw you."

"Well I thank you very much for your kindness," Thrifty says. "It'll be nice to have some company."

I'm about to walk away and leave Thrifty and Patch to their new lives together but before I get a chance to, a snooty looking female comes out the door of the house we're standing in front of.

I can't tell if she's white or one of those Black, Creole types that like passing for white. But, I am certain that she's a bitch on wheels.

"Thrifty, I'm not paying you to talk," she says. "You can go back to the corner if you want to have a conversation with some hoodlum. If you're going to be here you're going to work."

"Excuse me Miss..." I start talking and pause when I realize I don't know the lady's name.

"Sarah," Thrifty says.

"Who said I want this man to know my name?" Sarah says.

"Excuse me, Miss Sarah," I say. "I don't know what would give you the idea that I'm a hoodlum but you're way off bass here. You don't see any pants falling off of my ass or doo rag on my head. I look as respectable as I expect to be treated."

"Respectable... Huh," she says. "I'd appreciate it if

you'd just leave my help alone so he can get back to doing what he was doing."

"Actually, I was just about to leave," I say.

"Well, bye," she says. "You don't have to give me a speech."

I remember the line from the old school classic movie Cooley High. At that point I know that she's not white. She's a sister with an attitude that's just pretending to be white.

"Damn, the worst of both worlds," I think, "She has the attitude of a sister and the snobbiness of a white woman. But she is cute. Too bad. The world has more than enough pretty packaging on chicks that are rotten as hell on the inside. That's one wrapper I'll pass on opening."

Without saying anything else, I get in my car and drive off. In the back of my mind I think that Little Miss Sarah is a prime candidate for my next victim if I decide to choose one. She deserves to get played. And I'm just the type of man that would love to play her ass out.

***

I've had a happy three days without Patch. I'm just about back where I need to be mentally and my swagger as well as my confident disposition is both shining through.

It probably has something to do with the fact that today I'm meeting with the executor of Bongo's estate so that my claim to many of his riches can be made official.

I never really knew much about Bongo's family. I'm not sure he had any family. His dad adopted him and left him with a fortune. Why would he have done that if there were other family members to take care of?

The way that I see it, I 'm in the clear as far as getting Bongo's cheddar. At a minimum, I'm about to have absolute control over the DC and Arlington, Virginia shops. Today is a good day. Today is a good day indeed.

***

"Patch! What the fuck do you mean, Patch?" I yell. I feel totally dumbfounded by what I'm hearing.

"Do please try to keep it down," Mr. Riverton says. "As I was saying, Mr. Long was extremely clear with his directions. He's left the majority of his estate to charity. The remaining two- point-five million and his stake in the partnerships of his salon are to go to Patch. But, you needn't worry. You will be able to make reasonable draw-downs of the money on a monthly basis so that you can tend to Patch. The quarterly checkups at the vet for Patch are only procedural. I'm sure that you'll do a fine job taking care of him. As soon as you complete the first visit to the vet and get a copy of the results I'll be able to hand over the ownership certificates for his stake in the salons. I've given you the card and the Veterinarian says that she'll see you right away. I don't know what the problem is. Everything will work out just fine."

I leave Mr. Riverton wondering if everything will work out just fine.

My being able to find Thrifty the first time was pure luck. Who's to say that I'll find him again?

Maybe my chances aren't too good but I have to try. I'm not the type of person that accepts defeat well, especially without putting up a fight.

***

I drive around for hours looking for Thrifty. Not to mention that it's a Friday, my money day, so Melisa is calling my phone like crazy. I have clients out the ass today so even if she fills in with half of them they will still be a lot of them left hanging out to dry. Melisa's good but she ain't that good. Nobody can hook up a woman's weave as fast as I can.

I try to take my mind off the shop for a second and focus back in on looking for Thrifty. Something tells me to go back to the street where the snotty-ass woman named Sarah lived. It's a long shot but what else do I have to go on?

I spot Thrifty down the street from Sarah's house, in the same cull de sac where I saw him before.

He doesn't seem to be working with the same vigor as before. I wonder if he's sick. Or, he could just be starving. I'm sure that not many of the people that he worked for had the heart of Bongo. Bongo made sure that Thrifty was well fed and hydrated any time that he did work at his house. Now, Thrifty looked like he was operating on just fumes.

I blow the horn as I park and get out of the car. Thrifty looks up and acknowledges me.

"Hey… I don't remember your name," he says.

"Where's Patch?" I ask. "I came to see how he was doing?"

Thrifty's already sunken face sinks in some more.

"What's wrong?" I ask when he doesn't answer my question. "Wait. I hope nothing happened to Patch. Did something happen to Patch?"

"She took him," Thrifty says. "The day after you gave Patch to me she took him away from me. She said I messed up her yard and she was keeping the dog in trade for the cost of repairing it."

"You're kidding me, right," I say, not really to Thrifty. I'm really speaking to myself. "Well, we'll just have to see about this."

I jump in my car and peel off. I'm driving way too fast for the short distance that I have to drive but I'm beyond pissed.

When I screech to a halt in front of Little Miss Sarah's house, I'm pretty sure that smoke rises up from under the wheels of my car.

Incensed, I stomp up the driveway and bang on her door like I'm the Police. I can't seem to tone it down, not even after Little Miss Sarah opens the door.

"What's this about you taking Patch from Thrifty?" I ask. "I gave Patch to Thrifty to watch for me. You don't have the right to be kidnapping my dog. And Thrifty didn't have the authority to give him to you if it was of his own free will."

"Cut the crap, Mister," she says. "You don't give a damn about that dog. The only reason you're here is you saw the newspaper."

"What the hell are you talking about?" I say.

Now I'm dumbfounded.

"Don't act like you don't know that there was an article in the newspaper talking about how Bongo Long left millions of dollars to his dog," Sarah says.

It's starting to become clear to me. Sarah read the newspaper and that's why she took Patch from Thrifty.

"First of all, Little Miss Sarah," I say. "I don't know a damned thing about what you're talking about. And second, Patch is my dog so Thrifty or nobody else had the say so to give him to you."

"It's obvious that you abandoned the dog," Sarah says. "I told you the other day that I know a hoodlum when I see one. The only reason you're here now is you see dollar signs. And, you know what else? I really wish that I had time to sit here and quibble with you but I don't. Take this card. Anything else that you want to say you can say it to my attorney. My father always told me not to consort with criminals the likes of yourself."

Sarah shuts the door in my face after giving me her two cents about Patch. I want like hell to bang on the door again and curse her the fuck out but I'm quite sure that she'll call the cops. She may even have called them already. I glance down at the card and see Robert Sterner, Esquire. I try to decipher where I've heard the name before but I'm coming up empty.

Maybe my mind is too focused on the way that Sarah called me a hoodlum and criminal. I didn't take it as her showing prejudice towards me like so many people do nowadays. She sounded like she had personal knowledge of me as a person. I didn't know Sarah from Adam so how could she have acquired that knowledge?

It turns out that Robert Sterner is Sarah's father. Sarah is the younger of two children fathered by Robert, the other being her brother Thomas.

The reason why the name Robert Sterner seemed familiar to me the day that Sarah handed me the business card is her brother Thomas is a Private Investigator. But, he isn't just any Private Investigator, he's the one that looked up every piece of dirt that he possibly could on me for Bongo while he was alive.

It's been three months since Sarah handed me her father's business card. We've been going through one of the most grueling custody battles ever, for a dog nonetheless.

I really don't know how I'm going to win this case, either. I walked into the courtroom on day one feeling as cocky and confident as ever. But, with each day that passed I became more and more unsure.

Not only was my case unraveling, though. Everything with me has been unraveling.

I barely ever step into HBS now. I've put so much pressure on Melisa that she's the one that gave a stranger a chance just like I did with her years back. Melisa is supervising, doing marketing campaigns, and running my business just like it was hers.

HBS may possibly be the only thing positive that I have going for me in my life. The judge renders his verdict today and I'm already prepared for the worst.

"I find in favor of the Defendant, Sarah Sterner," the judge says. "She's awarded custody of the dog, Patch as well as the ownership interests held by Mr. Bongo Long in the DC and Arlington, Virginia locations of HBS."

I cringe as I hear the words. It's amazing that some stranger can come take some shit away from me that was one-hundred-percent mine.

"This can't be karma," I think.

I'm positive that once again the racist world has taken something away from a Black man that he's struggled to acquire fair and square.

Well, maybe it wasn't totally fair and square but I bussed my ass all the same.

This is fucked up. This whole shit is fucked up.

CHAPTER TWELVE

Breakdown

I vaguely remember having the nervous breakdown that I had the day after the judge told me I lost everything that I worked so hard for.

It's been nine months now and I'm finally back.

I wonder how things are going to be with Melisa. I told her that she's in charge until I get myself back together. I even gave her limited power of attorney over my business affairs.

I go to HBS early so that I can let the sights and smells of my business seep into my brain again prior to having to deal with my staff. I've had a peaceful time as of late and there's no way that I can just jump into the hustle and bustle of the noisiness in my shop during afternoon hours. I need barbers and stylists to show up one by one so I can experience the ignorance gradually.

I'm surprised to see the lights are already on when I put

my key in the door. As a precaution, I lock the door back after I enter and tiptoe around the shop trying to figure out who's already here.

Of course, it's Melisa.

"You used to argue with me tooth and nail when I told you to come in this early to cover for me," I say to Melisa's back.

"I'm used to it now," Melisa says. "You asked me to step up for you and I did. I've been stepping up for a long time now."

"So, what are you working on?" I ask. Melisa seems too focused on something other than me when I'm in the room.

"I'm looking over these papers that the attorney gave to me," Melisa says. "I'm actually glad that you're here. I was going to come past your place today to go over these. You should really think hard before turning this proposal down. I don't see you getting a deal any better than this."

I take the papers from Melisa and read them in detail. I can't believe what I'm seeing.

Sarah Sterner will be able to keep all profits from the DC and Arlington businesses but she will have to change the name from HBS. She gets to keep the building in Arlington but I get the building in DC. As far as stylists and barbers, they get to choose which salon or boss that they'd like to work for.

"So, I get a building but no money," I say. "Who negotiated this?"

"I did," Melisa says, hesitantly. "Actually it was more like a suggestion than a negotiation."

"I'm not being critical," I say. "Honestly, I'm surprised Little Miss Sarah budged at all. She's not the most compromising person I've ever met. If you think I used to be evil, you don't have a clue about the type of person she is."

"Used to be," Melisa says. "What does that mean? And why do you seem so different?"

"Different how?" I ask.

"I'm not sure," she says. "You seem so at piece. I know what it is. You're acting the way a woman acts when she's madly in love."

"Is that right?" I say.

"Yeah, so tell me who it is now, Fraser," Melisa says. "What's her name?"

"There is no her," I say. "But you are correct. I am madly in love. I'm madly in love with not just any man, the man."

"See, I knew there was something funny about the way that Bongo looked at you," Melisa says.

"Melisa, I'm not gay," I say. "I've never been gay and I'm definitely not gay now."

"Michael, please," Melisa says. "Why don't you try telling the truth for once in your life."

"What did you just call me?" I ask.

"I don't know what you mean," Melisa says.

"What did you call me?"

"I called you what I always called you," Melisa says.

"No... You didn't," I say. "I'm positive you called me something else."

"Fraser, look me in the eyes and tell me that you never had sex with Bongo," Melisa says.

"I can't tell you that," I say, deciding I need to come clean with Melisa. "But, I mean it when I say I'm not gay."

"How can you be with a man and not be gay?" Melisa asks. "Don't you know that God was clear about killing them and stoning them when he was talking about homosexuals?"

"God was also clear when he said 'let he that's without sin cast the first stone,'" I say.

"Well, at least you know something about the Bible," Melisa says.

"I know a lot about the Bible," I say. "But, don't change the subject. You never answered my question. You never told me what you called me."

"That can wait," Melisa says. "First, I need to tell you something that I never told you before."

I look at Melisa curiously. I can't imagine what she has to tell me after all the things I've been through over the past year.

"I thought it was funny when you told me that Bongo had you checked out," Melisa says. "It wasn't funny like humorous but it was funny because he had me checked out long before he did that to you."

"What? Get out of here," I say. "Why do you think he did that?"

"I'm sure it had something to do with Bongo being obsessed with you," Melisa says. "He made that clear to me the day he approached me with a file similar to the one you told me he had on you."

"Really, what did he say?" I ask.

"In a nutshell, he told me to stay away from you," Melisa says. "He said that if I didn't make trouble for him as far as you were concerned then he wouldn't make trouble for me."

"How could he make trouble for you?" I ask. "I was very clear with Bongo that this location didn't have anything to do with our partnership."

"He said that he would tell you where I was from," Melisa says.

"You always were ashamed of where you're from," I say. "Why is that?"

"I never said that I was ashamed of where I'm from," Melisa says. "I'm actually proud of where I'm from. I just didn't like to talk about it. I figured it was my business. I felt like I wasn't required to tell anybody where I'm from."

"So, do you feel the same way now?" I ask. "I'd like to know where you're from."

"Do you remember that hair and make-up competition?" Melisa asks.

"How could I forget," I say. "We won the whole thing running away. I did my thing and you won the make-up portion of the competition by a bigger margin than anybody had ever done. I still can't believe how good you are with make-up."

"Make-up has always been my thing," Melisa says. "You can totally change someone's attitude if you put it on right. You can turn someone into a totally new person."

"Melisa, why are we talking about make-up?" I ask. "All you've been doing is changing the subject today."

Melisa stares at me like she's seen a ghost. I feel a little creepy. But, I'm not as worried as I'd be if it were someone else. Because, I know it's Melisa, I think she's just trippin'.

"You heard right before," Melisa says. "And I want you to know that I forgive you."

"Forgive me? Forgive me for what I ask?"

Melisa starts pouring rubbing alcohol on a hand towel.

Once it's soaked, she begins wiping it against her face. Soon, she's massaging her face hard.

She has her back turned to me so I can't really see her good while she's doing what she's doing. But, I can tell that now she's left her face alone and started fumbling with her hair.

She plays and plays with herself for close to five minutes. When she's done. She turns around. What I see almost makes me feint.

"Like I said, I forgive you, Michael," Melisa says. "And to answer your other question, I'm from Jersey City, just below the Holland Tunnel."

I can't fathom why I'm standing in front of Miss Victim Number Two.

Does she have a gun? Is she planning on killing me? What exactly are her intentions?

"So, you found me?" I say.

"It wasn't easy," Melisa replies.

So many things that didn't make sense to me before start running through my mind. It's no wonder Melisa acted so much like Miss Victim Number Two. She is Miss Victim Number Two.

"Now I know why you didn't force me to wear a condom," I say. "I already infected you."

"I'm not the only one that you infected," Melisa says.

"I always wanted to know why you did it."

"If you would have asked me a long time ago I would have had a different answer than I can give you right now," I say. "I've been a victim my entire life. I never deserved half of what I got. Back then, I felt like I had to pay women back for the things that I've been through in my life. I had everything. All the women that I trusted took something away from me."

"So, you thought it was in your power to take something away from women indiscriminately?" Melisa asks.

"I can't vouch for my chain of thoughts back then," I say. "I can say that I'm sorry for doing to you what I did. You didn't deserve it."

"Do you think sorry is going to make everything better?" Melisa asks.

"What do you plan to do with me?" I ask. "Do you want to ruin me? Do you want to smear my name all across town? Are you gonna make me run away again, rebuilding my life someplace else?"

"Just like you, I don't know what my intentions are now," Melisa says. "I'm not even sure I knew what my intentions were back then. Honestly, I planned to put all of that bad stuff behind you until you said something about another man. I still can't figure out why you think you aren't gay if you sleep with other men."

"That was before, not now," I say. "And I don't consider a learned behavior to be gay. You can't judge me, Melisa. You don't know what it's like to grow up in boarding schools and juvenile detention centers. When people force themselves on you it is what it is. You accept it or you get hurt, maybe killed. And if you call yourself snitching and turning them in to the authorities your life will really be shortened. I learned to use everything bad that ever happened to me in my life to my advantage. So, don't call me gay. Don't ever call me gay."

"Ok, so you've explained your past, I'll give you that," Melisa says. "But, what does that have to do with you being in love with another man now?"

"This man is the best man I've ever known in my life," I say. "I wish I would have found a way to learn about him sooner. Things would have worked out so much differently for me. I've never known love like this was possible. Anger had clouded my judgment for years before I met him."

"Michael, I came here because I love you," Melisa says. "It wasn't about revenge with me. It isn't about revenge now. I looked past all the bad things on the surface of you and saw the person inside. That's the person I fell in love with. That's the person I would die for."

"Are you serious?" I ask. "Are you saying you wanted to be with me even though I gave you HIV?"

"You're the man that I fell in love with," Melisa says. "I told you before that I chose you. And you can't say that I haven't been patient. I stood by you. I believed in your dreams. I helped you when you weren't even able to help yourself. Now, after all that I've done and after putting my life on hold for years for you, after forgiving you for changing my life with this dreadful disease, you're gonna sit here and tell me that you're in love with another man. Then you play with my intelligence when you tell me not to classify you as a gay man. I don't think that all of the people you've killed over the years would buy your definition of your sexual classification. Bongo certainly didn't."

"I have done some things, some horrible things," I say.

"And I'll have to take that guilt with me to my grave. But, I know that I've been forgiven for what I've done. Before you forgave me God forgave me ten times over. And I am adamant about not being classified as gay. God took that away from me. God took all my terrible vices away from me. That's why the man I speak of being in love with is God. He's turned my life around. I never knew that all of the older women in the world were right when they tried to get me to give my life to him. Now that I have, there's a peace inside of me that no one can take away. There's a richness in my life that will never again become poor no matter how much money I have in the bank. I'm a new man. I'm the person that I always wanted to be and God has shown me how to be. That's why I've dedicated my life to that man. God has my undivided attention and devotion. He's repaired everything that was broken in my life. I'll never mistreat another woman again."

Melisa looks me up and down like she can't believe what I just told her. I wonder if my words have caused her to go in shock.

"When did all of this happen?" she asks.

"It was a gradual thing," I say. "After the judged rendered his decision in favor of Sarah I started going to Bongo's dad's church. I figured I can't keep hiding from the pain I instilled upon people. I knew the only way that I could change is if I had a firsthand reminder in front of me everyday of the devastation that I've caused."

"I wanted so bad to be that reminder," Melisa says. "I knew that deep down you weren't a bad person. I wanted to be there when you transitioned into the person that you were meant to be so that I could give you the love that you were yearning for when everything went wrong in your life. I see now that God has given you that love. But, that doesn't mean that he doesn't want you to have an earthly manifestation of the same type of love."

"God is all that I have," I say.

"God is all that we all have," Melisa says. "But, that doesn't mean that God won't put certain people in our lives. Why else would he have created Eve for Adam if he didn't know how much humans need companionship."

"How could I look at you in the eyes knowing what I did to you?" I ask.

"Michael, I forgive you and I love you," Melisa says. "You and I can start over together. No more eyes for eyes and teeth for teeth. Let's let God fight our battles. Let's take solace in the fact that God put us in each other's lives for a reason."

***

Given my past, I honestly don't deserve Melisa. Never-the-less, I'd be foolish not to take her up on her offer to be with her. They don't make women like that anymore. She was sewn together with a different type of cloth.

With Melisa's help, I was able to locate all of the victims whose lives I'd devastated or their families. I dished out over five hundred thousand dollars to them anonymously. I know that still does not repay the loss of a life or a terminal disease, but at least I tried to do something.

Melisa says me that I do not need to worry about the money.

"You've built the best salon that this area has ever seen so what makes you think you won't be able to do it again?" she had asked me.

I must say I have to agree with her. Besides, she's more help than both Freddie and Bongo put together.

I never thought that I would have the chance to have a good life, especially with a woman. However, when I opened my heart, let go and let God, everything has turned out just fine for me.

Moreover, the sky is the limit. With God on my side and Melisa in my corner, I am about to do bigger and better things. I will never sentence myself to failure again.

Preview a new novel by

Sidi

Daddy's Boyfriend

A novel by

Sidi

PROLOGUE

Melissa

It had been three weeks since Nikki had turned me on to our current girl-girl situation. Truth be told, this is the first time that Nikki has taken me anywhere. Even when it's time to eat, she always wants take out. It's like she never trusts me to leave her house — not even when I'm with her.

She looks so dutiful standing in line, ordering my food exactly how I want it. But I can't front, she's exactly the type of chick that I would have laughed at before if I were with some of my girlfriends.

Nikki is about five feet six inches tall, she's not too toned, and her features aren't that great. And honestly, she just looks irritating. But she's very caring. And she can charm the pants off of any chick.

But if you could compare Nikki to the chick two places behind her in line, it'd be easy for you to understand where I'm coming from.

The girl behind Nikki has a nice light caramel complexion, whereas Nikki is as dark as burnt toast. The girl behind Nikki has a nice, petite, movie-star nose to go along with her movie-star figure. I already told you that Nikki isn't exactly toned but I didn't tell you how spread out her nose is across her face.

The girl behind Nikki has plump, tender-looking breasts. She's probably a D cup. The only place on Nikki's body where she isn't too big but still found a way to be flabby is her chest. Sometimes I wonder if the bitch is just pretending to be a chick with a chest so flat. But she can't be. She has the same thing I have between her legs. I saw it.

Finally, the girl behind Nikki is swaying with class and purpose when she walks. It's almost as if she's floating on air. My God she looks heavenly when she moves.

Now Nikki, on the other hand, her dumb ass is just bebopping across the room looking.

***

"Bitch, you are gonna stop fucking disrespecting me!" Nikki says as she grabs my face hard and forces me out of my trance.

"Let go of me, Nikki!" I state forcefully.

But Nikki doesn't ever back down to the forceful tones I use like my husband Stevie did — or any other man that I've ever messed with in my life for that matter.

Whack!

My face stings like hell as Nikki starts berating me, making me feel like a child. I don't know why she doesn't feel like she's already embarrassed me enough after grabbing my face and smacking me in public.

"You ain't gon' be eyeing no other bitch up and down while we're out together," Nikki snarls. "I knew I shouldn't have let your ass out the house 'cause you don't fucking know how to act."

"Let, Nikki?" I ask, confused. "What the hell do you mean, let? I'm a grown ass woman. We've only been together for three weeks. You don't fucking own me! What part of the game is this?"

"This is the part where you respect me," Nikki says angrily. "That's all it is — nothing else. If you ever disrespect me again, we're gonna have problems."

I look into Nikki's reddened eyes and she honestly looks like a crazed maniac. It's been rough since Stevie got locked up but, truthfully, Nikki is scaring me right now.

I did what I had to do to get me and my baby out of the shelter but I'm wondering now if I did the right thing. My life is all messed up. And as bad as I need a dick right now I don't know why for the life of me I'm pretending to like pussy.

I reach for my plate to grab a fry and Nikki smacks my hand away. At that point, I remember why. The growl in my stomach is telling me that it's time to do damage control. I can't have my meal ticket all pissed off at me.

"I'm sorry, baby," I say sweetly to Nikki while rubbing on her bumpy ass face. "I didn't mean anything by what you think just happened. I was daydreaming, that's all. I'm here with you — you and nobody else."

Nikki stares into my eyes searching for sincerity. I'm sure that she can't find it. But you can't tell her that. I guess she wants so desperately to believe the bullshit I'm telling her that she finds truth where all there is are lies.

"Just don't do it again, baby," she says, calming down while leaning over to kiss me in the mouth.

"Blah, yuck, phooey!"

Of course she takes special care to stare down the goddess that I was just staring down as she's kissing me.

Oh well, I guess the dog of a bitch that I'm with to keep myself and my daughter off the street and out of the shelter has to mark her territory. But at least tonight my baby will have a hot meal when she comes home from school.

My life is hard right now but that's just the way I have to live it.

CHAPTER ONE

Daddy's Gone

Four months earlier in Harlem, N.Y.

Harlem, N.Y., famous for Malcolm X strolling up and down 125th Street, famous for poet and novelist Langston Hughes selling his books out of the trunk of his car, famous for launching the careers of countless entertainers who performed at the Apollo Theater's Amateur Night is also the place where nine-year-old Keisha Bey thrives in her own type of fame.

Keisha the only child of New York City's number one drug lord, Stevie Bey. So all the kids sitting on the stoop watching and all the little girls jumping rope with her right now consider her to be ghetto royalty. You don't cross her. You just try to (or pretend to) be her friend in the hope that one day she and her mother, Melissa, invite you on one of their shopping sprees. Just maybe you'll go home with some of the fly shit all the popular kids are wearing — as long as you stay in Keisha's good graces.

Keisha looks just like her mother. Many people tell Melissa that it looks like she just spit Keisha out all on her own.

Both are high yellow with a tint of a tan, long curly hair, lanky legs, and a fierce shape. Melissa teases Keisha by saying that she already knows what kind of rear end she's going to end up with.

"I guess I'm gonna have to beat those little niggas off with a stick in a minute," Melissa jokes with her daughter.

Both of their eyes are a captivating grayish turquoise. There is no proper name for the color.

As young as she is, Keisha is already growing bumps on her chest. Melissa knows that Keisha's will someday mirror her own full C cups. But no one knows that Melissa had a breast reduction a couple years back. Everybody thinks that her breasts got smaller because she started working out so hard.

Like her mother, Keisha is a picture of perfect health. She always wins at double-dutch. "No one can jump as long as Keisha does," they all say.

Today her talent is in question. Little Ramona Gregory from down the block seems like she just may outlast the neighborhood champion. All she needs to do is hold on for another minute or two.

"You got it, Ramona!" her cousin Twinkee says while popping on her chewing gum.

Twinkee's real name is Dashawneria but everyone calls her Twinkee because that's her favorite snack. Twinkee is also a lot easier to pronounce than Dashawneria. Many have tried to get her name right but eventually gave an up and just started calling her Twinkee.

"Twinkee, you know I ain't gon' beat Keisha, girl," Ramona says. "Are you trippin' or something?"

"Yes, you can beat her," Twinkee replies. "All you have to do is keep trying. Don't give up. You can do it. You'll see."

Ramona throws her leg into the rope and gets tangled up. Everyone moans awww because her jumping ended so close to Keisha's time. It was too good to be true anyway. No one can beat Keisha jumping double-dutch. No one.

"Are you serious, Twinkee?" Ramona asks. "What do you mean don't give up and I can do it? I know I can't do it."

"Yeah right," Twinkee says.

The um hmms from the other little girls tells Ramona that they all agree with her. They really think that she can't beat Keisha.

Ramona pulls her cousin aside so they can talk in private. She doesn't want what she has to say to be heard by any of the nosy little girls that jump rope with them.

"Twinkee, you really didn't notice that I let Keisha win?" Ramona asks her cousin.

"No you didn't," Twinkee says.

"Yeah I do, all the time," Ramona says. "And I don't thin I'm the only one. A lot of us just let her win."

"Why would y'all do that?" Twinkee asks. "That seems dumb."

"'Cause Ms. Prissy couldn't handle losing," Ramona says. "Look at her with her spoiled ass."

"I'ma tell Aunt Sue you're cussing so you'd better stop," Twinkee says. "And why would you be talking about your friend like that?"

"My friend?" Ramona asks, seeming shocked. "You think Keisha is my friend? I can not stand her!"

"You can't stand her?" Twinkee asks. "So why do you act like you like her?"

"Because she's ghetto royalty," Ramona says. "I can't tell the truth about not liking her. Everybody else in the neighborhood would treat me like I don't belong."

"I know that you don't want that to happen," Twinkee says. "But it still doesn't make any sense to pretend to like somebody. If I didn't like somebody, I wouldn't even want to be around them."

"Well, that's the difference between you and me," Ramona says. "You're living in a make pretend world and I know what time it is. Momma always tells me that you have to play the game in order to survive in this world. I need people like Keisha and her mom and dad to like me so things can be better for me. But that doesn't mean that I have to like her. I just have to pretend until her family goes down. Like Momma says, drug dealers always go down. It's just a matter of time. Then I'll be double-dutch queen of the block."

"If you say so," Twinkee says.

"No. I know so," Ramona replies.

*****

Inside a black Hummer in another part of Harlem, Keisha's father's driver, Vamory, frantically tries to elude the police.

Since they are dirty right now — meaning they have drugs and firearms in their possession — getting caught by the cops is the last thing that Vamory or Stevie want to do.

"Come on Vamory! Drive this motherfucker!" Stevie snaps. His almond colored skin is flushed and his deep, dreamy eyes are looking more than crazy at the moment. Vamory's bald head is covered with beads of sweat that drip down his massive neck and shoulders. He looks like he could compete in the World's Strongest Man competition, he's that buff. He is six foot six, two hundred eighty pounds of pure muscle, not an ounce of fat on him. He is in the enviable position of never having to worry about anything. No one ever even dares to knock Vamory off his center.

But today, Vamory can't seem to find it. He's feverishly trying to create distance between the Hummer and the cop car that is quickly gaining ground. Although both men are normally calm, being the two most feared men in Harlem, right now they are in a panic. They don't say the words but they are both thinking that the end of their long and successful run at the top the drug game is over.

"Vamory, you've got to do something!" Stevie hollers. "Drive up on the curb if you have to. We have more than five birds in this fucking truck today. And we got hella heat. Getting caught right now is not an option. This motherfucker is looking too serious to be on the take."

"Dammit, Stevie!" Vamory responds, sounding as irritated as he is. "You think I want to get caught? I'm trying to get away from this Jake! I don't know what the hell he has under that hood."

"Yo, you be mad if you want to be mad," Stevie says. "But you better remember who you're talking to right now. You need to watch your fucking tone, big nigga!"

"Stevie, I don't need this shit right now," Vamory snaps, not heeding his boss's warning. "It's not helping me to sweat me right now."

"Is that right?" Stevie says and pauses momentarily. "Yo, roll your window down."

Vamory doesn't understand why his boss wants his window down but he has too much going on right now to speculate. He presses the button and the electric window slides down.

Hopefully this will shut his ass up, Vamory thinks. Contrarily, Vamory is the one who goes speechless when the butt of Stevie's gun whacks him on his right temple.

He immediately loses consciousness and consequently loses control of the vehicle. The Hummer crashes into the fence of an abandoned lot and Vamory's body goes flying through the windshield. Today would have been the perfect day for wearing his seat belt. But since he didn't have time to strap it across his chest, he died as a shard of shattered windshield glass sliced open the carotid artery in his neck.

Stevie stumbles out of the Hummer with his hands in the air. "He was going to shoot at you. I grabbed the gun from him and was trying to throw it out the window. We struggled. After that, I don't know what happened!"

"Shut up and get down on the ground," the officer yells,

flying out of the police car with his gun drawn. "Get on the ground with your arms spread out and don't make any sudden moves."

"I told you, I ain't done shit!" Stevie says as he slowly makes his way to the ground. "I don't have nothing to do with none of his shit. The man was just giving me a ride."

"Save that story for someone who gives a shit," the cop says. "You're ass is going in today. At a minimum, you're going in for reckless endangerment and eluding a peace officer."

"I ain't elude shit!" Stevie says. "I wasn't driving! And how could I endanger somebody when I was in the back seat. I wasn't even riding shotgun!"

"And you won't be riding shotgun for a long, long time if I have anything to do with it," the cop says. He places a knee on Stevie's back. "Put your hands behind your back so I can put these cuffs on." He cuffs Stevie. "Are they too tight?"

"Hell yeah, they're too fucking tight!" Stevie yells.

"Good," the cop says, pulling tightly on the cuffs to ensure that it hurts Stevie even more.

*****

At the police precinct

"What is your name, sir?" the desk officer asks politely.

Mr. John Robinson, Esquire," Stevie replies. "His number is 917…"

"Wait a minute, sir," the officer says. "I asked you for your name not the name of some lawyer."

"Mr. John Robinson, Esquire, 917…"

Officer Harbaugh, the police officer who arrested Stevie, is becoming very agitated.

"This bastard is getting on my nerves," Harbaugh says. "I bet I find a way to make his ass come clean."

Harbaugh goes into the room where they are holding Stevie.

"Admit it, Bey," Harbaugh says. "You killed an innocent man to cover up the fact that you were in possession of all of those drugs and guns."

"I have no idea what you are talking about, sir," Stevie responds. "That wasn't my vehicle. I was just getting a ride. I had no idea what that man had in his truck."

"Bullshit," Harbaugh snarls. "You know more than what you're saying. Why don't you just admit it and save us all a lot of unnecessary time and headache."

"Did anyone hear me when I said John Robinson, Esquire?" Stevie asks. "I'm not even sure why y'all are talking to me right now."

"I'm tired of your bullshit," Harbaugh snaps, slapping the table where Stevie is sitting.

"Again, all I have to say is John Robinson, Esquire," Stevie says. "And his number is…"

"Yeah, I know," Harbaugh says. "It's 917, blah, blah, blah. Somebody get this piece of shit out of here."

Two officers escort Stevie to be processed. All the while, he's wondering how anyone could have known that he was transporting shit, something he hardly ever does anymore.

I smell a sheisty, dirty-ass rat, Stevie thinks. But I'm gonna find out who it is. Then that's gonna be a dead-ass rat."

CHAPTER TWO
Backtrack

As Stevie sits in the cell, he tries to retrace his activities over the past few days to figure out where he may have went wrong.

"How could anyone have known what was going down with Vamory?" he asks himself. "I did everything I was supposed to do. No one knew anything But but…the Pastor. I wonder if it's him?"

Stevie's mind drifts to the day five months ago when he bought the specially tinted windows for his limousine. They were supposed to be one-sided mirrors like those cops use in interrogation rooms.

"Are you sure that my chauffeur won't be able to see what I'm doing in the back if he decides to get nosy?" Stevie had asked.

"I'm positive," the mechanic had said. "You and your wife will have all the privacy you'll need."

"I wonder if I should have checked out the mechanic," Stevie says, reasoning with himself. "There's no way in the world that Vamory could have known about what was going on in the back of the limo. I made sure that the music was blasting so even if there was a wire in the car he couldn't hear shit. Something had to be going on that I'm not aware of. I just have to figure out what that is."

A correctional officer appears in front of Stevie's cell as he's sorting things out in his mind.

"Let's go, Bey," says the correctional officer. "Your attorney is here to see you."

*****

"So what makes you think Vamory was compromised?" Mr. Robinson asks Stevie. "And I wonder why the cops aren't treating him like scum the way they would any other criminal."

"You just answered your own question," Stevie says. "They're too damned interested in what happened to Vamory in the Hummer. But why? The only answer I have is that Vamory was about to snitch."

"Stevie, are you sure you're telling me everything?" Robinson asks. "What about what the police confiscated from the Hummer?"

"Vamory had to be trying to set me up," Stevie says. I've seen that nigga go one hundred thirty miles an hour without batting an eye. But the moment we're riding dirty, he decides to go the speed limit with the cops chasing us."

"So you knew that there were illegals in the car?" Robinson asks.

"I know now," Stevie says. "That damned Officer Harbaugh has embedded it in my brain. Now you've said it , too.

Of course I now know that there was illegal shit in that car."

"Stevie, I can't help you unless you level with me," Mr. Robinson says.

"Listen," Stevie says. "They cannot trace anything in that car back to me. Vamory was an employee of the limousine company. I paid for a tour of the city. I was simply a passenger who had nothing to do with whatever was in that vehicle. When the Jakes check shit out, they'll know that their only legal recourse is to let me go. They can't pin a thing on me."

"I just have one more question then," Robinson says. "Did you know that Vamory had requested police protection? Officer Harbaugh couldn't wait to tell me that Vamory was cooperating fully with the department. Why would he need protection? If we can answer that question, then things will start to make sense to both of us."

"The Pastor…" Stevie mumbles to himself.

"What was that?" Mr. Robinson asks.

"This has to have something to do with the Pastor," Stevie says.

"What makes you think that?" Mr. Robinson asks.

"Because he told me that there was something he needed to talk to me about but I've been busy for the last few days," Stevie says. "Maybe Vamory shook him up so he contacted the Fruit of Islam for protection. Maybe they stepped to Vamory and he felt in return that he needed the Jakes to watch his ass."

"Possible. But why would Vamory want to talk to the

Pastor?" Robinson asks. "What could he possibly say to a Pastor to shake him up? And why would the Pastor respond in a way that would make Vamory feel the need for police protection? There's too much going on here between a chauffeur and a Pastor for this to make any sense. Again, Stevie, I can't help you unless you come clean with me. You have to be forthright about everything or I won't be able to do a good job for you."

"You're right," Stevie concedes. "These past few months I've donated a lot of money to this church. I don't think Vamory was too happy about it. Religion wasn't necessarily his thing. That's all I can say for now. I have to finish thinking this through."

"Well, at least it's a start," Robinson says. "I think I'll go have a talk with this Pastor."

"I think you should," Stevie says as his lawyer hands him a pen and a piece of paper.

"Write his information down and I'll get in touch with him," Mr. Robinson says. Stevie does as he asks. "I'll be back in touch as soon as I know something."

Robinson leaves Stevie with a million thoughts running through his mind.

How much did Vamory know? Did Vamory tell anyone else? Did the Pastor speak to anyone?

"Onlyy time will tell," Stevie whispers to himself as the C.O. leads him back to his cell.

As the cell door slams shut, Stevie thinks back to the first time he attended the services of the now infamous Pastor he's so worried about.

He sat in the front row just as he'd been accustomed to doing at every concert or play he'd taken his wife to. He was adorned in a Brooks Brothers' suit that was cut perfectly. His designer silk tie cost more than the entire outfits of most of the other male parishioners. His Ferragamo shoes and Rolex watch caught the attention of every usher, deacon and female church member within viewing distance, Even the good Pastor seemed transfixed by the dollar signs emanating from Stevie.

With each crescendo in his sermon, the Pastor asked "Can I get a witness?" and turned to Stevie as if seeking his approval.

At the time, Stevie wondered how a man who appeared so young and untested could lead and direct such a large congregation, many of whom were more than twice his age.

The Pastor was very handsome, well-spoken and remarkably fit. Stevie surmised that if the Pastor ever got locked up, he would be the target of many of the male inmates — no matter which prison he served his time in.

Stevie often thought about how his wife had commented that the Pastor had a very sexy mouth. He'd always wondered what that meant. But as he looked at the Pastor's mouth with its full, perfect shape, the meaning became clear.

The Pastor had a fresh cut and shape up, including his moustache and beard. He sported a tapered goatee that drew attention to his striking facial features — most notably his lips, dimples, smooth skin and hazel-brown eyes.

As the Pastor raised his arms in the air to punctuate his points during his sermon, the muscles in his forearms were extra prominent. His tight veins revealed his passion, and the echoes throughout the edifice amplified his strength each time he struck his fist down on the podium.

The Pastor was extra theatrical that first sermon. It was almost as though he was auditioning, trying to do extra well just to show the man with the deep pockets that he'd found the right home to deposit his offerings.

He seemed to move with a purpose — to make sure that Stevie would notice everything he did.

What struck Stevie funny was that just as the Pastor knew that Stevie was hanging on his every move, the Pastor was also hanging on Stevie's every move.

It's fair to say that both men noticed that the other was noticing every tiny detail. In the concrete jungle of Harlem, both lions in their own right were posturing to claim the title of dominant male.

Stevie smiled in his cell as he remembered the end result of all the posturing.

CHAPTER THREE

The Beasts Within

"That was certainly an inspiring message," Stevie had said to the Pastor. "Something inside of me was moved deeply as you spoke."

"Glad to hear it," the Pastor had said. "Why don't you hang around for a few minutes. I'd like to talk to you. I just have to acknowledge some of the members first."

"Sure," Stevie had said. "I have a little bit of time to spare."

"Good," the Pastor had replied. "I'll just be a moment."

"Don't rush on my account," Stevie had said. "Sometimes you have to take your time with things."

The Pastor smiled deeply at that before he walked away, dimples more prominent than ever.

Most of the members of the church had cleared out by the time the Pastor found his way back to Stevie.

"I'm so sorry for taking up so much of your time," he had said. "Perhaps we could go talk to my study to talk privately. If I stay out here, I can't guarantee that another member won't take me away from you."

"I'm not that possessive," Stevie said jokingly. "But

maybe you're right. Going to your study may be the best thing."

"Allow me to lead the way," the Pastor had said before guiding Stevie into a room that some members had never seen.

Stevie and the Pastor spoke about tithing, the importance of male role models in the church, the church's expansion fund and many other obvious and safe issues.

But the topic both men tiptoed around was how each of them had been admiring the other.

Perhaps it is not politically correct for one man to say how much he appreciates another's swagger. Maybe it is because you almost never hear one man call another handsome. Whatever the case, both men remained tightlipped about how they felt about each other. It took Stevie stating that he was about to leave to cause the Pastor to speak up.

"Don't leave yet," the Pastor had said. "There are a couple more things I wanted to discuss with you."

"But we've talked about everything," Stevie had said.

"Not everything," the Pastor had replied.

"What else is there?" Stevie had asked.

"I just had to tell you that you are one handsome man," the Pastor had said.

"Is that right?" Stevie had replied.

"Definitely," the Pastor had said. "I know that most men try to act too masculine to acknowledge that another man is handsome. But I have no problem admitting it. If you've got it, you've got it."

"Well, you're not too bad yourself," Stevie had said. "I guess you've got whatever it is that you think I have."

"So," the Pastor had said uncertainly.

"So," Stevie had replied.

"Is it just me?" the Pastor had asked.

"Is what just you?" Stevie had asked in response.

"You're not going to make this easy?" the Pastor had asked.

"Make what easy?" Stevie had said. "The Bible says ask not, receive not."

"I think you mean ask and you shall receive," the Pastor had said.

"So ask then," Stevie had said. "Maybe you'll be able to receive whatever it is you're trying to receive. You never know until you try."

"It's just that… I mean… Things like this aren't easy to say because it's not like I feel the need to say them every day," the Pastor had said.

"Do you need help with something?" Stevie had asked while placing his hand on the Pastor's shoulder. The Pastor trembled. "Is something wrong?" Stevie continued.

"Yes, something is terribly wrong," the Pastor had said as he turned away from Stevie. "I rebuke you, demons."

As the Pastor looked up in the air as if he were talking to spirits that weren't of this earth, Stevie became more and more perplexed.

"Look, I don't know more about this stuff than you do so maybe someone else would be better at helping you," Stevie had said before taking a couple steps back as if he were about to leave.

"No," the Pastor had said before lunging at Stevie and kissing him squarely on the mouth.

During the moment of awkwardness afterwards, the Pastor stepped back far enough to avoid being punched in the face if that was Stevie's intention.

"Why did you do that?" Stevie had asked.

"Step back?" the Pastor had asked. "I didn't want to get mangled in my own church."

"I won't harm you," Stevie replied. "I want the same thing you want."

"Really?"

"Yes, really," Stevie stated. "I just wish you didn't spend so much time stalling."

"Well, let's not waste another second then," the Pastor had said.

"I won't," Stevie had said. "But to be clear, I'm a giver not a taker."

"Good, because I plan to take everything you have to give," the Pastor had said.

"Sounds like a plan," Stevie had said. "But I will allow you to give me one thing."

"Say no more," the Pastor knowingly replied.

In an instant, he pushed Stevie against his desk and feverishly peeled off his suit jacket. Seconds later, Stevie's tie, shirt and pants were history.

With his huge hands, the Pastor grasped both sides of Stevie's Sean John boxer briefs and pulled them down to the floor. He smiled as Stevie's manhood stared him in his face.

For the first time in his life, the Pastor decided not to fight his urges for and attraction to men. He eagerly took Stevie's manhood in his mouth and handled it with his jaws and tongue in the same manner he had instructed many women to do to his own over the years.

Stevie could not believe how good his dick felt. He could not believe that another man was making him feel that good.

Yes, Stevie had been with other men before but that was when he was locked up. Every thug knows that sex with men in prison doesn't count. What else are they supposed to do?

But as the Pastor performed oral surgery on Stevie's manhood, he had no excuse. He was as attracted to the Pastor as he'd ever been attracted to any human other than his wife. Before now, Melissa had been Stevie's world. She'd been the only person to ever make him cry during sex. Yet the way that the Pastor was making him feel at that moment was moving his wife to the furthest reaches of his thoughts.

"Suck it just like that," Stevie had demanded. "Goddammit, that feels good!"

Not wanting to stop doing what he was doing, the Pastor paused from massaging Stevie's balls so that he could raise one hand to point at the picture of Jesus.

"What? We can fuck in the church office but not curse?" Stevie had asked.

Without further objections, the Pastor continued to suck on Stevie, giving him the best blow job he'd ever had.

"Shit! You'd better stop," Stevie had said. "I'm about to bust off in your mouth."

"Don't," the Pastor had said quickly. "I want to feel it in my ass. I've always wondered what it would feel like to have hot semen in my butt."

With that, the Pastor stood up from kneeling in front of Stevie and removed his robe. Seconds later, he was bent down across the desk in front of Stevie with his naked ass in the air and his pants bunched up at his ankles.

Roughly, Stevie grabbed the Pastor's waist as he thrust his manhood inside of him.

"Ahhh!" the Pastor shouted as the excruciating but beautiful pain consumed his body.

Specks of blood formed around Stevie's penis as the Pastor was transformed from a heterosexual male into an in-the-closet bisexual.

With each powerful thrust, the Pastor became one with the pleasure-pain mixture of his first homosexual experience. He went to the place he'd always imagined but had never before had the gumption to experience. His life had been forever changed. From that point forward there was no turning back.

*****

Reminiscing about his first time sexing the Pastor brought back memories to Stevie. But they didn't help him figure out how Vamory could have known anything.

Stevie recalled that ninety percent of the time, he and the Pastor had sex in the study. The other ten percent of the time, they had had sex in the limo after he had had the special glass installed.

"There's no way he could have known," Stevie reasoned to himself.

Suddenly, a vision of an episode where Stevie was digging deeply into the Pastor's asshole came to mind. The Pastor was flailing wildly and inadvertently kicked some of the controls in the limousine.

"I wonder if Vamory was able to hear us?" Stevie asked himself.

The thought of someone as engulfed in his camp as Vamory knowing that he fucked another man made Stevie start to feel sick.

"That can't be it," Stevie said. "He couldn't have known. He better not have known. Shit will never be the same if he knew and told."

Also published by

Harlem Book Center

The World's #1 Best Seller

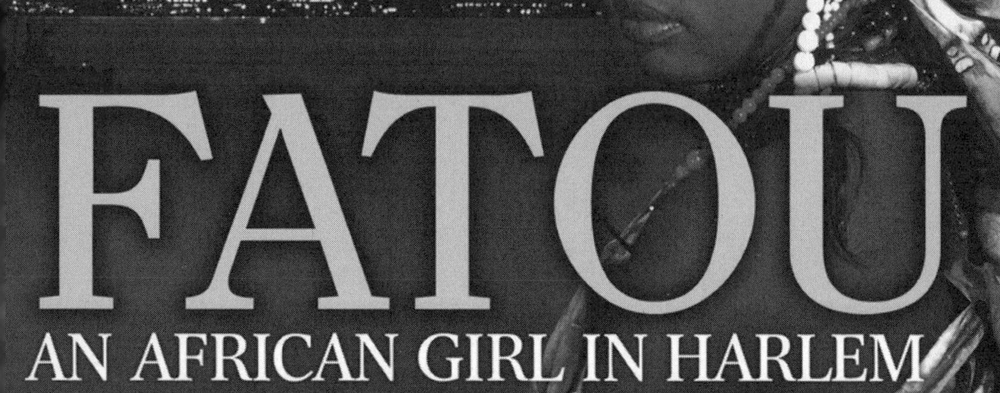

FATOU

AN AFRICAN GIRL IN HARLEM

By Sidi

A Novel

Fatou
An African Girl in Harlem

Twelve year old Fatou travels from West Africa to America thinking she's furthering her education. Yet, she arrives in New york City greeted by a man three times her age—someone from her village who paid a dowry to be her husband. Suffering through pedophiles, deplorably cruel living conditions, and a slave-life job eventually pushes her over the edge. When the smoke clears, she refuses to be a victim and exerts control of her life by becoming part of Harlem's fast money scene. The resulting terror leveled at anyone who gets in her way doesn't mask her old wounds but it does soothe her overwhelming hunger for revenge. Aside from money, power, respect,and her new love for New York city's number one drug lord, that's all a West African girl in Harlem has to look forward to.

This fast paced novel examines what happens when the bonds of family and tradition fall apart. And it shows how a strong and fearless woman can hold her own surrounded by grimey men in the dangerous drug game.

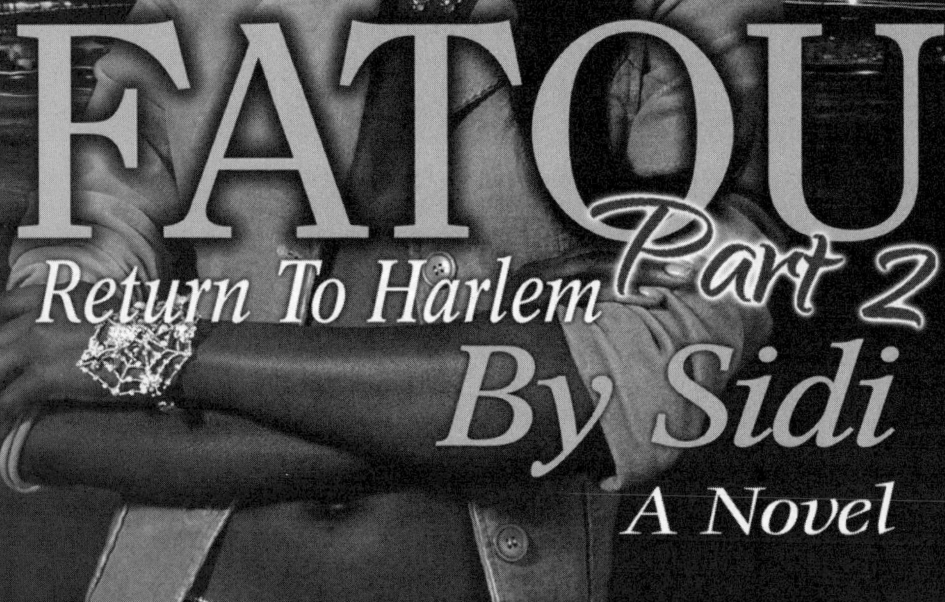

The World's #1 Best Seller
FATOU
Part 2
Return To Harlem
By Sidi
A Novel

Fatou Part 2
Return to Harlem

With the love of her life mysteriously murdered, West African Harlemite Fatou sets out to discover which of her murdered lover's lieutenants in New York City's most notorious drug cartel was responsible for setting him up. After finally getting to a peaceful state in her own life despite suffering through pedophilia, rape, being kidnapped, and working under slave labor type wages, the death of the man that picked her up when she was down finally pushes Fatou over the edge. And, although the lieutenants mistakenly assume that the death of Fatou's lover will soften the reigns of her control, they find out that he was the one that had previously cooled her down when she was about to blast off. There will be no such luck now that Fatou is on her own and poised to exact revenge. Everyone around her will find out what happens when a woman with an attitude is in control and determined to get respect one beat down at a time.

The rage in this story of revenge is furious and shows you that you'd be better off antagonizing a ravenous pit-bull than to get on the wrong side of the wrong woman. Beware everyone because Fatou is back with a vengeance. I advise everyone to duck, put down your shades, and close your curtains. Don't be caught in the path of her wrath.

The Lesbian's Wife

A Novel By

SIDI

BEST SELLING AUTHOR OF FATOU

The Lesbian's Wife

For her twenty-first birthday, Aisha (Nikki) Kone receives the surprise of her life—an all expenses paid trip to Africa from her father, the esteemed Muslim leader, Fah Kone. Finally, she believes, he has come around to her way of thinking and their strained relationship is on the mend. But nothing could be further from truth.

Nikki's father has never accepted his daughter's "alternative" lifestyle, one of the greatest sins in the Islam religion. And he has his own selfish plans for her future.

With the memory of the love and devotion of her partner, Beyonce, a constant reminder of the life she used to lead, Nikki survives kidnapping, rape, beatings and starvation. As her life becomes a living hell as her world is turned upside down, Nikki uses her Harlem street smarts and her killer body to stay alive. And through it all, she secretly plots to exact revenge against her father and against her kidnapper, one of the most powerful men in the Ivory Coast.

MANDINGO

THE GOLDEN BOY

By SIDI

AUTHOR OF FATOU, FATOU 2 AND THE LESBIAN'S WIFE

[illegible]

Mandingo — The Golden Boy

Sex for sale will never again be the same for one reason. Mandingo.

New York City's elite, the power brokers in business and government, have it all – power, money, respect and the very beautiful Denise Jackson to indulge their sexual fantasies. To pay her way through college, Denise sells her luscious body not only to them but to the lonely wives of those powerful men.

When she meets Mandingo she sees the opportunity to increase her profits. Mandingo is a magnificent specimen of a man. And after sampling his fifteen-inch tool, she trains him to be her biggest moneymaker.

In addition to his natural gift, his bedroom savvy and expertise keep his clients coming back for more and more. And after personal tragedy strikes, the money Mandingo earns almost makes up for his decision to go against his morals and become a male prostitute. But to make matters worse, he falls hard for Denise.

Life is good for Mandingo until things spiral out of control. Women close to him start dying, the police harass him, Denise rejects him. Ultimately he is arrested for a murder he did not commit. His cushy life suddenly becomes a living hell and all the best sex in the world can't put right what has gone wrong.

This erotic thriller and murder mystery is a page-turner, sure to heat up many nights and stimulate all the senses.

MANDINGO

THE GOLDEN BOY

PART 2

By SIDI

AUTHOR OF FATOU, FATOU 2 AND THE LESBIAN'S WIFE

Mandingo — The Golden Boy Part 2

African immigrant to America, Mandingo has warmed the beds of many women during New York City's chilly winter nights. Yet he didn't know — or care — that many of them were married with children. Eventually he finds himself in a world of trouble, facing deportation and even the threat of losing his life.

But Mandingo isn't oblivious to the dangers ahead of him. After surviving a previous murder attempt, he told himself that he would be more careful. Yet with so many women throwing themselves and their rich husbands' money at him, the words are easier said than done.

Mandingo received a blessing from God in the form of a new lease on life. But when his thirst for money, fame and the mind control he has over the women he beds cause him to go fishing in a pond of women married to the most powerful and ruthless men in New York, will he be able to close the can of worms he opened?

Ride on Mandingo's wave of sex, money and mayhem. Experience the chill of his manly prowess and the thrill of him trying to avoid the punishment his enemies have in store for him. Then learn if Mandingo's over-the-top sex game can bring him the luck he needs to survive any and all pitfalls or if riding the dangerous wave of adulterous sex will finally make him wipe out once and for all.

the Streets of Harlem

BY LESTER MARROW

The Streets of Harlem

Lester Marrow grew up on the streets of Harlem during the drug epidemic that plagued the ghettos of New York City, and beyond, and defined the post-VietnamWar era. The Streets of Harlem is his real-life account of growing up in one of the roughest neighborhoods in the country.

In his matter-of-fact style, Lestoils (as many of his friends called him) tells the story of the drug game with brutal honesty and in graphic detail. He nostalgically recounts vicious childhood memories but flavors them with the bitterness of regret and resignation. His autobiography chronicles drug deals and near-arrests, murder sprees and sexual escapades, getting money and lots more money. And then losing it all to reckless drug addiction.

Throughout his life, Marrow's one constant love was music, and The Streets of Harlem is rich in the musical memories that accompanied many of his illegal and dangerous activities. Marrow was right there at the birth of hip hop and rap and tells how it all began.

The Streets of Harlem is truly a gripping story because it is REAL. Marrow's memories of his experiences will shock, terrify and frighten — and ultimately make you feel as if you lived those days right along with him.

Tamika
The Struggle of a Jamaican Girl

At age nine, Tamika Jefferson adored her father Marley. He was basically her world. But when he was arrested on trumped-up charges, she quickly learned that her world would be turned upside down.

Tamika is ignored and neglected by her mother who seems to care more about receiving her green card so she can permanently stay in the United States than protecting her daughter from the unwanted advances of a boyfriend who continuously lies about marrying her so she can become a naturalized citizen. At one point, Tamika's mother even suggests to little Tamika that she needs to grow up and do what she has to just as her mother has been doing things for her.

Get lost in this gripping tale about how the system fails to protect young Tamika from those that would do her harm yet doesn't hesitate to punish her when she finally defends herself. And find out how far Tamika's alter ego, Tammy —who shows up inside of Tamika's head during the years of abuse — will go to protect her when no one else will.

This story follows Tamika from her early years of being abused to her life after being released from prison for the murder of her accuser to taking over her father's illegal business to ultimately becoming the leader of the notorious Unity of Jamaican Brothers crime syndicate.